Confessions from the Principal's Chair

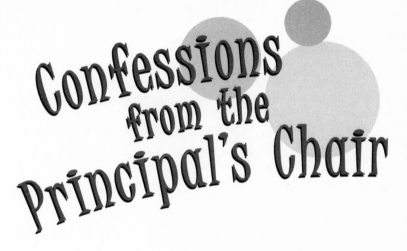

Confessions from the Principal's Chair

ANNA MYERS

Walker & Company
New York

First published in the United States of America in 2006 by
Walker Publishing Company, Inc.

For information about permission to reproduce selections from
this book, write to Permissions, Walker & Company,
104 Fifth Avenue, New York, New York 10011

Library of Congress Cataloging-in-Publication Data
Myers, Anna.
Confessions from the principal's chair / Anna Myers.
p.   cm.
Summary: After participating in a cruel prank, her mother moves
them to Oklahoma, where fourteen-year-old Robin is mistaken for the
substitute principal and gets to see a new perspective on bullying.
ISBN-10: 0-8027-9560-9 • ISBN-13: 978-0-8027-9560-1 (hardcover)
[1. Bullying—Fiction.   2. Schools—Fiction.   3. Friendship—Fiction.
4. Mothers and daughters—Fiction.   5. Oklahoma—Fiction.]   I. Title.
PZ7.M9814Co 2006   [Fic]—dc22   2006001970

Book design by Donna Mark
Visit Walker & Company's Web site at www.walkeryoungreaders.com
Typeset by Westchester Book Composition
Printed in the United States of America by Quebecor World Fairfield

2 4 6 8 10 9 7 5 3

All papers used by Walker & Company are natural, recyclable products
made from wood grown in well-managed forests. The manufacturing processes
conform to the environmental regulations of the country of origin.

• • • • •

This book is dedicated with love to a group of very special people: my nieces and nephews. I am certain your grandparents in heaven are as proud of you as I am.

Ed and Dena Kephart, Josh and Kacie; Becky Kephart and Palmira Campos; Lisa and Dr. Mike Pruett, Sarah, Chris, and Luke; Amy and Dr. Robert Trent, Laura, Margaret Grace, and Rob; Emily Biggers; Tracie and Marshall Godfrey, Austin, Alisen, and Leslie; Jason and Tonya Hoover, Kyzor and Kinzer; Ross Hoover.

Laurie Scrivener and Joe Soliz; Greg and Joy Scrivener, Andy, Meredith and Ethan; Holly and Ryan Meck; Wendy and Tom Knight; Cody Flora.

• • • • •

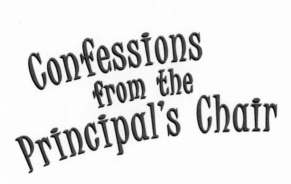

Chapter 1

So do you want to know how I ended up in the principal's office? I mean really in the principal's office, not in the chair across the desk where kids land when they are in trouble. Believe me, I've been in that seat plenty, but not this time. This time I was the principal! Yeah, that's what I said, me, Robin Miller, but BTW most people don't call me Robin.

See, Rendi (she's my mother) jerked me out of school in Denver. "I've had it, Bird!" she yelled at me soon as we were in our van after leaving the counselor's office, where they had made a big deal over a little teasing. "I don't want you being part of the Six-Pack anymore." She did that thing with her mouth, lips pressed together real hard like she always does when she's mad. Normally, she gets that look when she's fuming over someone who has a dog tied up without any shelter from the cold or because some oil company had a spill in the ocean or something.

Ordinarily she's laid back with me. She never carried on over the blue streaks in my hair or how I would only wear orange or lime green pants to school. "Your clothes express your personality," she said. "You get to choose."

Oh, sure, she got kind of quirky when she found out the other members of the Six-Pack also only wore lime green or orange pants. "I wish you would think for yourself instead of being a follower," she said back then.

"I do think for myself," I said. "I started the color thing. I can't help it if they copied me." Okay, maybe that wasn't exactly the truth. Okay, okay, that was a lie. Of course the pants thing had been Ivory's idea. Usually I didn't lie to Rendi, but back then she usually didn't push me into it.

"Well," she said, "I suppose you will grow out of it." Then she laughed. "Those pants are so tight, you're bound to grow out of them."

I remembered all that, sitting there in the van, Rendi with her lips pressed tight. Just stay cool, I told myself. I looked out the window, and I tried to keep my voice soft, but firm. "They're my best friends, Rendi. You can't expect me to stay away from them."

"You will." She reached over, took my chin in her hand, and turned my head so she could look me straight in the eye. "We're moving," she said. "They will have to call themselves the Five-Pack from now on."

"Moving! Rendi, we can't!" I said, but I was scared. See

* * * * *

the thing is, my mother is a sculptor. She can do that work anywhere. When I was younger, we moved a lot. Before I started school, we lived in three different states and eight different cities. After I started taking classes with Miss Deirdre (I'll fill you in on her later), we stayed around Denver, but we never bought a place. We'd move at least once a year, so changing schools happened a lot. Two years ago, though, when I was in sixth grade, we had this big talk, one of Rendi's meaningful "Look deep inside yourself, Bird, and tell me what you feel" talks, and decided to settle down in Denver. The idea was to stay put in one school district until I finished high school.

I should have known Rendi would get all worked up when she heard about what happened with dopey Marcy Willis. Rendi is always for the underdog. I didn't even try to tell her how Marcy brought all her troubles on herself. It would have been a major amount of talk that wouldn't have done a bit of good.

Still, I thought she'd come around. Rendi always listens to me if I give her time. We've got this really good relationship. I know because I've seen what goes on between some of my friends and their parents. Ivory practically hates her own mother, and sometimes they don't say a word to each other for days.

I'd always thought I had an awesome mother, which sort of made up for the fact that I can't come up with anything at all in the father department. A time or two

* * * * *

when I've been in trouble at school, some counselor has tried to bring up my father, like not having one is some kind of big deal or something. Well, it isn't, believe me. I don't even think about him unless someone brings him up, and that doesn't happen very often. Okay, okay, the truth is I do carry the little picture of him Rendi said a long time ago that I could have. She came across it in a drawer. I think she must have burned all the others or something. I mean there were bound to be others, don't you think? Anyway, I've got that snapshot in an envelope, and I usually keep it in a folder in my book bag. I don't think that means that I am troubled because he left us, do you?

I can't remember a single thing about him. Well, how could I? He dumped us about the time I was learning to use the potty chair. He was a painter (on canvas, not houses). Wait, I guess I shouldn't say *was*, like he is dead or something. I guess he is still a painter, although I sure haven't seen any pictures by him in the art shows I am always going to with Rendi. I haven't seen a penny of money from him either.

After a few years, Rendi went to a judge, and she got it all legal that he didn't have any right to come back into my life and start being all fatherish or anything. She even had my last name and hers changed to the name she had before she got married. Personally, I don't think she had to worry about him rushing back into my life, but I also think that it is good that I would recognize him, I mean because of the picture, if I should see him in a restaurant or something. Anyway, I think I would recognize him.

As far as I can tell, I got three things from my father. Number 1 is that I call my mother Rendi. That's what he called her because her name is Renee Dee. Her parents always called her both names, which I guess is real common where she grew up, the two-name thing, I mean. Rendi says my father sort of made fun of the double names and started calling her Rendi, as a combination. When I started talking, I picked it up from him. Now most everyone calls her that, and she even signs her work that way.

Number 2 is that wherever he is, he is tall. Me too. I've got these really long legs. Well, my arms are long too, and my body, and my neck. Isn't that awful? Oh, don't think I'm ashamed of being tall. That would be so last century! I'm glad to be tall, and I've heard that guys really like girls with long legs. So far the boys I've known have not seemed to be really crazy about my legs. The last boy who said he loved me was Jon McBroom in third grade. We were so wild for each other that we pulled each other's teeth at recess. The thing is, my tooth came out really easy. Pulling Jon's tooth wasn't easy, believe me. It turned out that Jon's mother came up to school and made a big deal out of the fact that his tooth wasn't even loose. Rendi got called too, but she said a third grader couldn't pull a tooth that wasn't ready to come out. See what I mean about how she usually sticks up for me. Anyway, Jon was my last ardent admirer (I got "ardent admirer" from a book, and I am praying that some sweet day I will have one again). Not really likely with my neck. I am certain boys don't have crushes on me because of my long neck.

Rendi says that I don't have a long neck. She even took me to a big deal hairdresser woman who said girls with long necks should wear their hair long and full, so the neck isn't so noticeable. My hair was already long and not doing much to help in the neck department. Oh yeah, and the hairdresser woman said my neck wasn't unusually long at all. Of course, I knew that wasn't true. I mean, I can see myself in a mirror, can't I? I guess some people like to be lied to about their hideously flawed bodies. I do not like to be lied to about mine, and I wear turtlenecks all the time except around the house. For a while, I thought maybe I could have plastic surgery, but I have looked on the Internet. I have not found any mention of plastic surgeons who cut your head off and make your neck shorter. I guess my only hope is that by the time I have the money for such a surgery there will be major advances in the area of cutting off heads.

The third thing I got from my father, who BTW was, no, *is* named Richard, is that I can draw really well. Some of Rendi's friends say I should be a painter too, but I am not going to be, and that isn't because I resent Richard or anything if that's what you're thinking. It is because I am going to be an actress. My acting coach says I'm good, and someone even more important than Miss Deirdre said the same thing too. I'm not going to tell who that someone is, though, because that would be getting ahead of the story, and speaking of the story, I probably shouldn't have been going into my whole life history thing.

Okay, I'll get back now to how Rendi and I were sitting in our van and not feeling especially warm toward each other, with her threatening to move us and being all worked up over Marcy Willis and everything.

She started the engine, and I slid down in the seat, thinking I'd just sort of stay far away from Rendi, be real quiet and make her want me to talk. I folded my arms across my chest and kept my eyes turned down toward the floor of the van.

So the looking down thing is why I didn't realize Rendi had not taken the street one block from the school, the same street we use to get to our house. I didn't know that she had gone a whole different way until I felt the van slow down and turn. I lifted my eyes to see where we were stopping. In front of me was a big sign that said, "Box Store" and a smaller sign that said, "Boxes—50¢ and Up."

I can tell you my vow of silence got forgotten as quick as yesterday's history lesson. "Boxes!" I said, "Rendi, can't we talk about this?" I touched the little can, a charm I wore on a chain around my neck. All of us Six-Packers wore that charm. What would I do if Rendi really made us move? She turned off the engine and held the key in her hand.

"Nothing to talk about," she said. "Got to have boxes to move." She opened the car door. "Come on," she said to me before she got out. "There will be too many for me to carry."

I considered screaming. Not only had my mother completely lost her "let's talk about it" attitude, she was making me carry the boxes, sort of like, you know, carrying the cross they meant to hang you on. I didn't scream, though, because I still thought I could get her to change her mind if I stayed calm.

Rendi bought the boxes, and I *did* help carry them. I helped pack them too. Except for some things in her studio that she arranged with a friend to ship when we got resettled, we got rid of most of the big stuff and took only what we could put in our van. The rest Rendi gave away to her friends, some charity, or weird people she found on the street.

"Don't bother to pack those crazy pants," she told me when she came into my room the first time. "We will be buying you all new school clothes when we get there."

"Would it be asking too much for you to tell me where 'there' is?" I didn't try to keep the sarcasm out of my voice. I mean, I could see my mother was actually going through with this awful move. "I bet there's some kind of

• • • • •

child welfare person or something that would make you not treat me this way," I said. "I'm not like some kind of criminal or something. I think it's child abuse to just drag me off without even telling me where we're going." I laid the stack of underpants I had in my hand down on a box that was turned upside down.

Rendi didn't comment on the abuse thing. Instead, she walked over, picked up the stack of underpants, handed them to me, and said, "Pack these. You'll need them when we get there." She turned to walk out, but just before she got to the door she turned back to say, "Bird, I don't know where we're going. We'll know when we get there." She shrugged her shoulders. "We'll start looking in Oklahoma."

"Oklahoma! Where Grandma and Grandpa live?"

"They live in Tulsa," Rendi said. "I think we need a little town." She closed the door behind her then.

I wanted to collapse on my bed, but it was gone. Rendi had put a sign on the corner that said, "Free Furniture," with our address and an arrow pointing our way. Two odd-looking women in long, dark dresses came in, took my bed apart like it was made of Lego blocks, and carried it between them, one piece at a time, out the door and loaded it on a trailer that held a lawnmower. One of them had a heavy shadow of a beard and walked like a man, and I kind of thought the other one moved like one (a man) too. I can tell you that I felt pretty strange watching bizarre strangers carrying off my favorite reading spot (not even to mention the place where I used to feel so comfortable and safe during snowstorms). Rendi, though, felt zero concern for my feelings. Oh yeah, she just chatted to the women-men about how we were going to have a real adventure. The short one made comments back to Rendi (the one with the beard didn't talk at all). Rendi held the door for them each time they went out. I watched from the front window as they threw my mattress on top of the lawnmower.

But I was telling you about how shocked I was to hear where we were headed. Since my bed was gone, I flopped on the floor to do some thinking. Oklahoma! I couldn't believe it. I never in my life would have thought Rendi would ever want to live in that state. I could just about count on the fingers of one hand how many times we had been there.

My first memory connected to my grandparents starts with flying there when I was maybe five or six. It was the first time I'd ever been on an airplane. Even though it was eight or nine years ago, I could remember it clearly and my grandfather's face too when I saw him at the airport, his dark eyes just like mine and the way his whiskers felt on my face when he kissed my cheek in the morning before he shaved. I liked my grandmother too, but it was my grandfather I took to most.

Rendi didn't seem to like either of them. She was quiet and kind of wound up tight, like she might just break into crying or screaming any minute. We only stayed two nights, but even a little kid like me could see that they were two too many days for my mother.

I saw how Rendi mostly made up excuses not to go to Oklahoma when her parents would ask us to come. If we did see them, the visit was short. Last spring we went for a couple of days, and I saw my grandmother once looking at Rendi when we were having breakfast. Grandma's face had the saddest look on it.

I did not mention that observation to Rendi. She would just have started telling me again about her parents, how they hadn't wanted her to marry my father and hadn't wanted her to be an artist. Rendi claims my grandparents have never approved of anything she has done. Maybe it's so, but personally I'd think they would be over any objections to her art by now. I mean, Rendi sells the stuff she makes for really good money. She has a piece in lots of important places, like airports and stuff. I kind of think maybe Rendi needs to forgive her parents for having doubts about her art, and, of course, they were right about Richard. Maybe that's what Rendi can't forgive them for, being right, but I am not claiming to be some kind of TV head doctor like Dr. Phil.

Maybe Rendi wasn't really born to my grandparents. Maybe she got mixed up with another baby in the hospital. I mean that's possible, right? She doesn't look anything like my grandmother, who has every hair in place and fingernails that are always perfectly manicured. My grandmother wears suits and dresses that are made by some important designer whose name you would probably recognize if I could remember what it is. Even when Grandma puts on casual clothes, they are classy looking. Her figure is perfect too. She could wear a two-piece bathing suit except that, of course, a woman her age wouldn't look proper in one. Grandma doesn't do anything that is not proper.

Rendi isn't what you'd call fat, but she isn't the type who should wear a two-piece bathing suit either. Her hair is really shiny and soft, but kind of plain, just light brown and pulled back by a loose ribbon. I've never seen her wear makeup, not even lipstick, and there is usually clay or something from her work under her fingernails. Still, Ivory really got me mad once when she said, "Your mother would be pretty if she did something with herself." Of course, I didn't say so to Ivory, but I like Rendi the way she is, or at least I used to before she turned on me over Marcy Willis.

So there I was on the floor of my room that had one chair from the kitchen and a chest left in it. One of Rendi's friends wanted the kitchen table and chairs. Rendi had tried to give the women-men the chest, but the one who talked said, "No, thank you." Anyway, like I said, I was on the floor wondering what it would be like to live in Oklahoma. Would my grandparents show up at our place uninvited, or maybe the whole family would kind of sit down and talk things out. Before Marcy Willis, Rendi had been a believer in talking things out. Don't ask me why she hadn't ever talked things out with her own parents. Maybe things would have been different if my Aunt Jenny, Rendi's sister, had lived. Rendi was really close to her sister, but Jenny died in a car accident when she was sixteen and Rendi was my age, fourteen. I'll bet Aunt Jenny would have made my mother work on her relationship with their parents, but, hey, I had a lot bigger problem than wondering why Rendi didn't get along with her mother and father.

I was about to get stuck in some brand-new school. I rolled myself into a fetal position (I read that in a book), you know, like a baby in the womb. I remembered what it had been like when I started middle school, me not knowing anyone from before and walking down those halls all alone. In elementary school, the halls had been friendly, even in new schools, but I can tell you middle schools do not have friendly halls. In elementary, the halls are all decorated with frogs and rabbits and pictures of presidents and stuff. Not in middle schools. Those halls are like prison halls, except I guess they don't have lockers in prisons. Anyway, I've never seen any lockers in prison movies, but I can tell you that the eyes that watch you in middle school halls are just as unfriendly as the eyes of all those murderers, rapists, and thieves. Those eyes (you know, at middle school) are as cold as the steel the lockers are made

* * * * *

from. Wait a minute, I'm not sure that the lockers are made of steel. Maybe they are tin, but then, I guess you get the point about how cold the eyes were when I started middle school in Denver.

Ivory had the seat in front of me in history. I could see that she was the coolest girl. She is tall, but not as tall as me. The thing is, though, that her neck isn't long at all. She could be a model or something, and she held her head up high, kind of like she might own the place or something. I guess you could say she does sort of own the place.

She isn't a cheerleader or on the pom-pom squad or anything. She's not that kind of popular. She's the kind of popular that doesn't need to do anything to earn it. I'm willing to bet every kid in the whole, huge eighth grade knows who she is. But stay with me here. I don't want you to get confused. We were in the sixth grade when I first met her. She asked me a week or so after school started if I had an extra pencil, and I gave her the one with the pink stripes on it even though it was my best one. "You can keep it," I told her, "you know, for later."

I liked her because of the way she looked and because she always nodded at me when she slid into her seat just before the bell rang. I knew why she was always nearly late and everything. I passed her every day in the hall with a group of other girls. They'd have their heads together, talking as fast as they could. Anyone could see they were good friends. I remember wishing I belonged to a group like that, with people who would always tell me their secrets and always be ready to walk down those cold halls with me.

It was like I had some kind of fairy godmother or something who had just been hanging around with her wand to grant my wish because, I'm not making this up, the very next day after the pencil thing, Ivory stuck her hand back toward me just when Mr. Simons started talking about how early Greece influenced life today. There was a note in her hand, and I got so excited that I forgot to hide what I was doing when I leaned down to get it.

"Robin Miller," Mr. Simons said, "can I please have your attention?" I honestly think that might have been the first time a teacher ever called me down, well anyway since second grade, when I let the class frog out of his glass cage. The teacher yelled at me then, but of course that day with Ivory sure wasn't the last time. After the day of the note, I got in plenty of trouble, for passing notes, being late to class, once for smoking cigarettes in the girls' room, and finally for teasing stupid Marcy Willis.

That first note from Ivory said, "No party here. [That's how Ivory starts every note, unless of course something really interesting is happening to her as she writes.] Do you want to hang out with me and my friends? We want to call ourselves THE SIX-PACK, and we really need another person. Tell me after this BORING class is over. Ivory."

• • • • •

That's how I got to be part of the group whispering to each other in the hall, and that's when the halls stopped being a scary place.

But now back to the packing. All the while, I kept hoping Rendi would come in and say, "I've been unreasonable. I can see that now." At around six, she knocked on the door. Here it comes, I told myself, and I also thought how I'd be forgiving. No use holding a grudge. My mother usually does so much better than the mothers of my friends. I could even forgive her for giving away my bed. It would be kind of fun to shop for a new one.

"Come in," I told her, but she didn't open the door.

"It's time to eat," she said. "Come and have a sandwich with me."

I definitely was not hungry, but I thought I caught a soft note in the sound of Rendi's voice. Maybe she would admit her error while we ate. "Okay," I said.

She had already made tuna fish salad, my personal favorite, especially when she puts in onions, and she had just to please me. She likes it better without onion. Sometimes she makes up two different batches, but not this time. I saw her take the stuff for both our sandwiches out of the same bowl. I sat with my shoulders hunched to show how miserable I was, and that I wasn't going to be bribed with onions. I took tiny nibbles off the edge of my sandwich.

"Bird," Rendi said after she had chewed her first bite. "I'm sorry that you see this as a punishment."

Wonderful! It was about time she started on the "I am sorry" track. I let go of a long sigh and turned my eyes to her with the saddest look possible. I mean, it wasn't a pretend sadness. She was about to drag me away from the best friends I had ever had. "How else could I look at this, except as a punishment? It *is* a punishment, Mother, a cruel and unusual punishment." I was proud of the part about cruel and unusual because I was pretty sure there was some kind of law or something against cruel and unusual. I was also using "Mother" instead of Rendi. I don't know why, but I thought it was a good tactic.

Rendi didn't seem impressed. "It isn't a punishment, although you certainly deserve to be punished for what you did to that poor child. We are moving because I think it is best for you. I think small-town life will do you good. You need to meet new kids, learn not to be a follower, learn to think for yourself." She reached over to brush the hair away from my eyes. "Remember how much fun we used to have, just driving down the road until we found someplace we both liked?"

I rolled my eyes and looked up like I was just about to pass out with disgust.

"Puh-leeze, Mother," I said. "In the first place, I'm not some ignorant little kid anymore. I can assure you, we won't find a place I like, not that it matters to you. I like it here. Besides, we picked on Marcy Willis for her own good.

Someone had to show her how pathetic she is. It's like a no-brainer to see we did her a favor."

Rendi didn't say anything else, just ate her sandwich. I picked at mine for a while, then got up, ran back to my room, slammed the door behind me, threw myself on the floor, and cried into my pillow (generously not given away by Rendi to the two weird people). The tears were real enough, but I took my face out of my pillow, and I scooted over to open the door too. Rendi needed to hear how she had broken my heart. I cried, and I cried.

It worked. In almost no time, she was knocking at the open door. I decided to play it sweet this time. "Come in." I raised my face just enough so she could hear me, then dropped it back, this time into the pillow. I could afford to be comfortable now.

Rendi came over and got down to sit beside me. She reached out to touch my hair, sort of wrapping a strand around and around her finger. "Bird," she said, "I hate to see you so unhappy." She started to tousle my hair, which is a thing that has always felt good to me and helped me relax. "Just think how it will be to go to school in a little town. You will know every kid in your class, and, oh, think about acting. They will be amazed at how good you are. You'll have the lead in every play, and we'll look for a place that has a nice little community theater. Why, you could even end up giving acting lessons to younger kids. Wouldn't that be fun?"

Rendi knew what would appeal to me. I didn't want her to know I was interested, but before I thought about it, I raised my head just a little. I realized real quick what was happening, and I dropped back against the pillow fast. It would be fun to give acting lessons. I'd been studying acting at Miss Deirdre's Studio since I was just a little girl around five. Miss Deirdre is an actress who used to be this big deal on Broadway. She starred in all sorts of plays with famous people, but then she was in an awful car accident. She lost the use of her legs. I guess there aren't a lot of parts for people who can't walk, so Miss Deirdre came to Denver and started an acting school. She said looking at the mountains made up some for not being a star anymore.

I started off in a class with some other little kids. They mostly couldn't even talk loud enough to be heard and couldn't even really pretend to be rabbits or elephants. Let me tell you, I could do a really mean elephant impression, my arm all drawn up to my face and waving like a trunk. I guess my bunnies must have been good too because it wasn't any time until Miss Deirdre told my mother she would like to give me private lessons, and that she wouldn't even charge us. Everybody said how good I was, and I had just packed away all sorts of trophies I got for being actor of the year at Miss Deirdre's school. Just a couple of months ago, Miss Deirdre told my mother and me that I could be in movies or on the stage in New York right now. She had called Rendi and said that she would like to talk to her privately about my future, but Rendi said I should come along. I heard her tell Miss Deirdre that she didn't keep secrets from me, that we discussed everything and made decisions together. Boy, that turned out to be a big joke, didn't it?

Anyway, Miss Deirdre said she still had some connections that would help me break into movies or plays in New York. Rendi turned to me right then and said, "Well, Bird, do you want to give it a shot?"

"We'd have to move, huh?"

"Yes," said Miss Deirdre. "You would have to move to the coast, either east or west."

We were in her office, Miss Deirdre behind her desk and Rendi and me on the love seat across from her. "Would I still have to go to school?" I asked.

"Yes," said Rendi.

"Well," said Miss Deirdre. "After you got a good-size role, arrangements could be made for you to be taught on the set, but I suppose it would be best to enroll you in a public school at first."

I looked down at the floor, wrinkled my eyebrow, and pretended to think. I didn't want Miss Deirdre to feel like she had wasted her time with the talk, but I knew right off I would say no. I loved acting, but there was no way I was going to go to a new school. Being part of the Six-Pack gave me security. No one would ever hassle me, and there was always a place saved for me in the cafeteria, even though we weren't supposed to save places there. Everyone knew not to take a seat meant for a Six-Pack member. No one was that brave or that dumb, except, of course, that brainless Marcy Willis.

Well, back to the part where Rendi was sitting beside me and moving my hair around on my head. "Hey," I said, and all full of hope, I sat up. "If you really want to move me, let's go out to Hollywood and let me try to get into movies."

Rendi shook her head. "No, Bird. I'd like to say yes to that, but I think I've been wrong about some things. A small town might be just what we need. Maybe my folks are right about how I've raised you. Maybe I should have been more conventional."

I wanted to protest then, to tell Rendi that she had been right to talk things out with me and to trust me to make my own decisions, but it wasn't a time I wanted to be agreeing with her. The phone rang, and she got up to answer it.

"Hello," she said, then she put her hand over the mouthpiece. "It's Ivory. I'll give you privacy so you can tell her good-bye."

I sat up and stared at her. This was real! Rendi was going to drag me away from Ivory and my four other good friends! I started to shake.

"What are you doing?" Ivory asked.

* * * * *

"Nothing," I said. Of course, it wasn't true. I was packing to leave my whole world behind, but we always started every conversation the same way, the "what are you doing, nothing" routine. "What are you doing?"

"Nothing," said Ivory. "How come you left school right after we got out of the office?"

"Rendi was real steamed," I told her.

"Rendi?" Ivory was surprised. "My mom gave me a big lecture and everything, but Rendi usually keeps her head. What'd she say?"

I sighed. Might as well tell her right out. "She says we're moving. We've been packing ever since we got home." My voice broke then, and I started to cry.

"Moving?"

"Yes," I said. "Rendi thinks I'd be better off in a little town, maybe in Oklahoma."

"No way! You're kidding me, right?"

I choked back my tears. "It's true. We're leaving tomorrow."

"What about us?"

I was a little disappointed that Ivory hadn't sympathized with me first, but then I decided it was natural that her number one thought would be how much they would all miss me. "I know," I said, "I'll be lonely without you all too."

"Who in the world will we get to take your place?" she said. "I mean, she'll have to have blond hair, and I don't actually know that many blondes."

We always talked about how there were three blond girls in our group and three girls with brown hair. A thought came to my mind, and it gave me a funny little feeling in my stomach. "That's just the way it worked out with me and all, wasn't it? I mean, it was an accident that the last one to join the group happened to have blond hair, right?"

"Bird," said Ivory, and she sounded a little disgusted. "You know I take the Six-Pack very seriously. I mean, we liked you and everything, but, yes, we did need a blonde. Now you're going off and leaving us with only five."

I studied the pattern in the little rug I sat on. She's just surprised, I told myself. In a minute she'll start to talk about how much she'll miss me. "We can e-mail each other every day," I said.

"Yeah," she said. "Hey, you won't be here for Halloween. I can't believe your mother is making you move before Halloween. She knows we've been planning that party at your house for ages. We've already told everyone, and I think Tyler is just about to ask me to be his date. Now where can we have the party?"

My feelings were getting seriously hurt. Ivory made it sound like I couldn't be excused to move until I found a girl with blond hair whose mother would let her have parties at her house. I didn't say that, though, because I never spoke up when Ivory hurt my feelings. It happened pretty often, but I overlooked it. After all, I knew I was lucky to be part of the Six-Pack.

●　●　●　●　●

"It's a while yet until Halloween. You've got time to find a place for the party," I said.

"I guess," Ivory said. "Well, I feel just awful about you moving. Your mother has sure turned mean, hasn't she?"

I had been thinking exactly the same thing, but somehow I couldn't just agree. "I guess she really does think it is best for me," I said.

"Well, she's wrong," Ivory said.

"Very wrong," I agreed. Neither one of us seemed to have much more to say, and Ivory hung up pretty soon, after we promised to e-mail each other every day. I tried not to think that she was getting out last year's yearbook so she could slide her fingers through the pictures to find girls with blond hair.

Next I called Felicity, but her mother answered and said she was grounded from the phone. I started to tell her that I was moving and would she please tell her daughter, but I knew she had recognized my voice, and she didn't sound at all friendly. Felicity's mother never really liked any of us much.

When Katie answered the phone at her house, I didn't even say hello or go through the "what are you doing" bit. "I'm moving," I blurted out.

"Moving?" she said. "Did your mother decide to buy a house?" Rendi had been thinking she might buy a place instead of renting, and I had told my friends.

"No, this is a major move, out of state, even." Katie started to cry, and I was so glad.

* * * * *

"I hate it," I said. "At first I thought I could talk Rendi out of it, but I can't. We are really leaving. I'll be going to some new middle school, alone, and walking to every class by myself."

"Oh, have you told Ivory?" said Katie. "We'll miss you so much."

After I hung up the phone, I called the other Six-Packers, Taylor and Stephanie. Both of them said they'd miss me and e-mail every day, but I couldn't help but notice that they both asked right off if I'd told Ivory, like I had to get her permission or something.

By the time we went to bed that night, what we planned to take with us was in boxes, and most of the rest of our belongings had been hauled away. Rendi always told me that things didn't matter, only people, but I felt lonely without our furniture. We slept that night in our sleeping bags on the floor because Rendi gave the Salvation Army her bed and our fold-out couch too. She always said that was one of the problems between her and my grandmother. Rendi gave away an expensive TV Grandma bought her once. Well, I was beginning to side with Grandma. Rendi was giving away my life.

Chapter 2

There wasn't much talk between Rendi and me after we got in our box-filled van. I stared hard into the mirror outside my window until Denver, the Mile-High City, disappeared. Back when I was a little kid when we left a place, I was always sort of excited. Now I was just scared and really mad! I had my backpack on the floor in the front with me. We hadn't been away from Denver long before I pulled my bag up and started rummaging through it.

"What are you looking for, sweetie?" Rendi said all light and friendly like she didn't know I was furious with her.

"Paper." My voice was as cold as I could make it.

"Good," she said. "I think it would be a good idea if you kept a journal as we travel, sort of record our adventures and your feelings."

My idea had been to start a letter, one to send in the snail mail to the Six-Pack minus one. I thought I could send it to Katie, and write on the envelope that she should take it to school, open it, and read it all together. I tried not to think about how there would be a new member. She wouldn't be interested in my letter. Deep down I wasn't sure Ivory would be interested either.

I took out a big pad of yellow paper. We all used that kind of paper for notes we wrote in class. A yellow pad was the most important thing we carried. We couldn't send each other a text message in class because our school had a rule against cell phones in class. If a teacher saw one, the phone could be taken away from the kid and never returned. Not even one of the Six-Pack could risk losing a cell. Yet, here I was in this prison of a van without one. Rendi had taken mine away from me, saying we'd be changing our service in Oklahoma anyway. I didn't start a letter, though. Rendi's idea came to my mind. I wasn't about to start some gooney journal about traveling around looking for some dumpy little town to live in, but I sure could write about how I felt. "PLEASE HELP ME! I'M BEING KIDNAPPED!" I wrote it in big letters, over and over across the page until it was filled up. I pushed down hard with the pen as I made the letters, and I liked the feeling.

On the second page, I started in on Rendi. "Who is this woman?" I wrote. "She claims to be my mother, but I have never seen her in my life. She is so strange to me. My mother would never treat me this way. What has this

• • • • •

woman done with my mother? I miss my mother. We used to talk over everything. I remember how she would say that she would never try to run my life the way her parents had tried to run hers. My mother thought I was smart and could think for myself. I wonder if I will ever see her again. I loved my mother like she loved me, but now I am this woman's prisoner."

Most of the way through Kansas I wrote on my yellow pad. Even when I just repeated the same thing, I liked doing it. When we stopped to eat, I would carry the pad with me and put it on the table between Rendi and me. I wanted her to read it. Moving was a done deal, but at least I wanted her to feel bad about the agony she was putting me through.

She never even glanced at the writing. Once I pushed it over closer to her plate than mine, but she didn't look at it. "I would never read your journal, Bird," she said like she didn't know I wanted her to read it. "I would never invade your privacy that way. That's the kind of thing my mother used to do to me when I was young."

I jerked back the pad. "Did your mother ever drag you away from your friends and take you to some foreign country to go to school?"

Rendi shook her head. "No, she did not, but I would have loved it if she had. Oklahoma is not a foreign country, Bird. I wish I could afford to fly us to some other country, so you could be exposed to a completely new culture, but I can't. I think you will learn something, though, from small-town life. I think you will like living in Oklahoma. New experiences make you grow inside."

"Yeah," I said. "Getting that tooth filled last month was a new experience. I know it made me grow."

Rendi didn't say anything, and I pulled a book out of my bag. It was one that should have gone back to the school library. I forgot that it was in my bag when Rendi went up to school to give back the textbooks and check me out. I guess they would have known about the book because of the computer and everything, but Ivory had picked it up for me and carried it out of the library without checking it out.

Mrs. Evans, our librarian, had told me when I saw it on the counter that I couldn't have the book because there was a waiting list for it, but when she went to stop a fight between two boys and take them to the office, Ivory stuck the book in her bag. "You'll have it read before she starts to look for it," she had said. I could have read it in one evening because I do love to read and won't put a book down until it's finished even if I have to let my homework go. I like Mrs. Evans, and I was going to take the book back that same day without telling Ivory, but I didn't get a chance to before we got called to the office. The book looked good, but I was too upset over what was happening to be able to read. Let me tell you, that has never happened before.

* * * * *

"Oh, that's a library book. We'll have to mail it back to them," Rendi said. "I hate that we took it, but at least you will have something to read."

"I can't read," I said. "It makes me sick." (That wasn't exactly the truth, but I liked the sound of it.) "Never happened before, but I guess this is the most sickening trip I've ever been on." I turned my head away from her and stared out at the flat countryside. I would never have admitted it to Rendi, but I liked the openness of the land and sky. It felt real strange to be in the car with Rendi and be so quiet. We used to talk a lot. I thought it must seem strange to her too, and I figured it was bound to make her feel bad. Well, good! I wouldn't talk to her for the rest of my life unless I had to. This time I'd keep my vow, like some kind of monk or something who lived in a monastery and never spoke a word. I didn't utter another sound even when we finally stopped for the night just before we got to the line between Kansas and Oklahoma.

"This place look all right to you?" Rendi asked when she pulled off the interstate highway and stopped at a motel. I only grunted, and I was proud of not saying a word all evening. The next morning we were back on the road again. We hadn't been in Oklahoma long before I saw a sign saying it was one hundred miles to Oklahoma City. I wondered about Tulsa because that's where my grandparents live, but I didn't ask Rendi. Monks don't break their vows that quickly.

* * * * *

When we saw a sign that said, "Ponca City—Exit One Mile," Rendi announced that she had been to that town once to visit a college friend whose family lived there. "There's a wonderful statue there called *Pioneer Woman*," she said. "I want to see it again, and I think you will love it."

I didn't even grunt. After we got off the interstate highway, we had to drive twenty-two miles to get to the town called Ponca City. Rendi chattered all the way, telling me how Ponca was the name of an Indian tribe. I didn't listen much, but I couldn't help liking the land, all open and sort of pulling you in to it. I didn't tell Rendi that I noticed anything good.

It was truly impossible, though, not to act interested when we stopped at the statue. Rendi just got out of the car without saying anything at all to me. I could see it, this really gigantic woman with a Bible under her arm. She's got on a sunbonnet, and she is walking, and she has her son by the hand. I didn't want to get out, but I actually swear to you that this woman called to me, like practically by name.

So I had to get out and walk over there. The deal is, I've looked at lots of works of art with Rendi. It's this thing that I've learned from her to love. She knew that statue would soften me up. "My great-grandmother was a pioneer in this state," she said, "like that woman, and you know what, Bird, we are like that." She pointed with her head to a nearby museum building with the words "I see

· · · · ·

no boundaries" written in big letters across its top. "You and I, we see no boundaries."

I guess I might as well tell you that the whole *Pioneer Woman* thing got to me. I stared up at her, and it was like I was seeing my great-great-grandmother, and I understood how she felt walking across that flat, open land. "She's beautiful," I whispered. It wasn't much talk, but I had just broken my vow. I knew if I stayed, I might end up going over to stand by Rendi, maybe even lean against her. I stomped back to the van, mad, mostly at myself. Rendi stayed awhile with the woman, then joined me.

"What a thrill that lady must have been for the sculptor," she said when she got back into the van. I knew she was thinking about her work. It had been a few months since she had done a special project, and I knew she was hoping one would come along. I didn't say anything. We didn't go back to the interstate. We just followed a small highway that went through Ponca City.

Pretty soon I saw a sign that would have made me laugh if I had been in a better mood. It said, "Prairie Dog Town fifteen miles."

Rendi saw the sign too, and she said, "Oh, good. Let's go there."

Since I had broken my vow of silence already, I thought I might as well express my disgust. "You want to see some dog that lives on the prairie? Don't expect me to get out of the car this time, no way, and I really mean it."

"Prairie dogs aren't real dogs," Rendi said. "They are members of the rodent family, sort of like squirrels, except they live in groups in holes they make in the ground. People call their holes prairie dog towns, but this Prairie Dog Town is the name of a little town for people. I've heard of it, but I've never driven through it. It might be the kind of place we're looking for."

"Rendi!" I screamed, and I do mean screamed. "You aren't thinking we might like to really live there? Surely you wouldn't live in a place called Prairie Dog Town! I'd be embarrassed to send any of my friends a letter with that return address."

"We won't stay unless we both like it," she said. "But what could be the harm in looking?"

I shrugged my shoulders. "If it amuses you," I said, real snotty like. She won't go, I told myself, but she did. It was true. I did not know the woman who drove this car and claimed to be my mother.

No one at my school in Denver would have believed Prairie Dog Town, Oklahoma, even existed. I knew better than to expect a mall, but this place was like something from a century ago. There was hardly a business district, just a little town square with a few buildings around it. I saw some little dumpy café, a hardware store, a grocery store, and one big sign that said "Feed and Seed."

"There's not even a Big-Mart," I said, then I thought of something that I knew would end the possibility of living in Prairie Dog Town. "Rendi," I said, "this place doesn't even have a library or a book store."

Rendi put her eyebrows together, thinking. "You know Ponca City isn't far, and they will have a nice-sized library. Blackwell isn't far either," she said. "And I just remembered that when I went home with that friend from college we saw a nice play in Ponca City. It would be easy for me to drive you there."

I put my face in my hands. "You promised we wouldn't stay unless we both liked it," I reminded her.

"Oh, we won't, but let's just go back to that café and have lunch, maybe drive around a little after. You might like it better than you think."

"When pigs fly," I said.

We stopped in front of City Café. Crazy name I thought. How could anyone call this place a city? I would have liked to refuse to get out, but I was too hungry. The mother I once knew would have carried out food to me. This new woman, though, was not likely to do that. The thought made me remember my yellow pad. I bent down to where I had stashed it behind my backpack and got it, planning to take it in with me. Maybe I would change my mind and make some notes about Prairie Dog Town, Oklahoma. It might give me something funny to e-mail my friends about.

A woman stuck her head out of the kitchen when we came in. "Just put yourself anywhere that suits you," she said. "We aren't too busy today."

I looked around. Not too busy seemed like a real

understatement to me. There were about six booths in the place, and only one of them had anyone in it. A dark-haired girl who looked a little older than me was putting food on a table in front of three gray-haired women.

I thought Rendi would head for the empty booth on the other side of the room, but she settled in right behind the old ladies. I wanted to die. What if she should start talking to the women all folksy-like? I could just imagine her telling them that we might decide to settle down in Prairie Dog Town, and they would be sure to make a joke about how the middle school needed a new little prairie dog. I had no intention of joining the rodent family.

The girl came over and handed us menus. She was chewing gum and making a popping sound with it. Rendi ordered a chicken sandwich and some lemonade. "I'll take a burger," I said without even looking, "and a latte." Of course, I knew they wouldn't have a latte. But I thought it would be funny to order one, like I expected that they served them all the time.

"What's a latte?" the girl asked between pops of her gum, and I laughed out loud.

"You mean you've never even heard of a latte?" I was truly surprised. I was about to say she must have lived in a prairie dog hole her whole life, but Rendi didn't give me a chance.

"A latte is coffee with steamed milk," she said, "but never mind. Just bring my daughter lemonade too."

I looked out the window at nothing until our food

• • • • •

came. The gum chewer slammed down my plate in front of me. Rendi smiled at her, and I knew she would leave the girl a big tip because she thought I had been rude.

We were about to pay when suddenly a tall, skinny man in a policeman's uniform and a huge white hat burst through the door. With his hand on the gun at his side, he stationed himself by the door and moved his head very slowly from one side to the other, searching the café like a gunfighter about to meet his enemy. I could almost hear the music from the old western movies I had seen. It was a minute before I noticed the yellow pad under his arm. A funny feeling started in my stomach. That pad looked just like the one I had been writing on, but didn't all those yellow pads look alike? What had I done with mine? I hadn't brought it in like I had planned. It must still be in the van.

I was standing beside a window near the cash register, and I moved the white curtain to see our van. There it was, doors closed just the way we had left them. Then I remembered! The pad had been in my lap when we stopped. I had taken it off my lap and laid it back on the floor or somewhere before I opened the door to get out, hadn't I?

The man came slowly toward us. "Hello, Barney." It was the woman in the kitchen, and her voice came from a window behind the cash register.

"I've asked you to quit calling me that, Judy. My name is Clyde," said the man. "You ought not be calling me any first name, let alone one that is meant to poke fun at me. I am the sheriff, and I think I deserve a little respect."

"Don't get your panties in a wad," said the voice. "I mean, hello, Sheriff Walters. Just settle yourself someplace. I'll get that piece of coconut meringue pie I saved you from earlier."

"Can't," the sheriff said real sharp and quick. "I'm here on official business." Out of the corner of my eye, I saw the woman come out of the kitchen, but mostly I was watching the sheriff, who was walking straight toward us.

The dark-haired gum chewer behind the cash register quit moving her hand with our money toward the drawer. The sheriff stopped right in front of us. "You two get out of that blue van?" He used his head to motion back toward where our car stood outside.

"Yes, officer," said my mother, "we did. Is there a problem?"

The sheriff started to draw his gun, but it seemed to be stuck in the holster. When he moved his left hand to pull at the holster, the yellow pad fell to the floor near my feet. I looked down to read my message, "PLEASE HELP ME! I AM BEING KIDNAPPED!"

By the time I looked up, Barney, or whatever his name was, had his gun out and it was pointed directly at my mother. "You are under arrest for kidnapping," he said. One of the older women screamed. "Hush, Aunt Margaret," said the sheriff, and he started to pull at the pair of

* * * * *

handcuffs he had attached to his belt. He launched into his speech about my mother's rights too, all the time pulling at the handcuffs. Rendi tried to say something, but he waved his gun at her. "You let me have my say," he told her, and he went back to the beginning of his speech and started over with "You have the right . . ."

I wanted to laugh, but I didn't think the sheriff or Rendi would see the humor in what was happening. I opened my mouth to explain that I wasn't being kid-napped, but the sheriff started talking to the waitress. "Angie," he said, "you come over here and get these hand-cuffs loose and put them on this low-life woman."

"Now wait a minute, Barney," said the woman named Judy who was now beside us in her apron and smelling like fried chicken. "Tell me what's going on here."

The sheriff stomped his foot. "You be careful, Judy Richardson, or I'll haul you in for disrespect to an officer of the law. We've got a desperate woman right here in Prairie Dog Town. I can only thank the good Lord I in-tercepted her before she got totally away with this poor child."

Angie had the handcuffs off of the sheriff's belt by then, and she was moving toward Rendi. "Hold your hands out, woman." He waved his gun, and Rendi put out her hands. "Be careful, Angie, this woman is violent."

I made up my mind then to tell the truth. I mean, I was mad at Rendi, but low-life and violent were going a bit too far. "Sheriff, sir," I said. "This is my mother. I wrote all that stuff about being kidnapped because I was mad at her."

The sheriff gave me a long look and made a sort of snorting kind of doubtful grunt. "You poor little thing. You've started siding with your captor. Not uncommon in kidnapping cases. In the law business, we call it the Stocking syndrome. I just saw a special about it on TV."

"Stockholm," said Judy. "It's Stockholm syndrome, Clyde, named for a city in Sweden where a famous kidnapping took place. I saw that same special."

The sheriff sighed. "Don't make no real difference what you call it, now does it, Judy? The point is that this pitiful little girl has been kidnapped and got her mind taken over by the scum that done it."

"Bird," said my mother, "tell this man the truth."

I looked at my mother for a long minute, and I started to wonder what they did with kids who had been kidnapped. "Sheriff," I said. "Will you send me back to Denver? I don't know what happened to my mother, but I've got a friend there named Katie Morford, and I am pretty sure her parents would take me in if you explain that my mother can't be found."

"Bird!" Rendi yelled, but just about that time Angie snapped the cuffs around her wrists.

"Silence, woman!" said the sheriff. "I demand silence." He turned to me. "Don't you have a daddy, child?"

"He left us when I was just a baby, and he didn't want

to pay child support, so we don't know where he is. My mother didn't try to find him because she said she could take care of me by herself, and she did until I was kid-napped." I looked down at my feet. Rendi *had* always taken care of me by herself. I never went without anything I needed and most of what I wanted. I was beginning to feel a little bit bad about what was happening with my mother. The woman who used to be my mother would have been able to laugh about it and enjoy telling the story when it was all over, but I wasn't so sure about the Rendi Miller who stood there in handcuffs. She was giving me looks that would scare most eighth-graders, but in some ways I am braver than most girls my age.

"Officer," said Rendi, and I could tell she was working at controlling her voice when she really wanted to scream. "I have this child's birth certificate in my van. Her name is Robin Diane Miller. I am her mother, Rendi. No, wait a minute, Renee Dee Miller is my real name, but I go by Rendi."

"So you have an alias, do you?" The sheriff nodded his head.

"No, I am a sculptor who works under the name Rendi. I have a small piece in the van. Just look."

The sheriff was studying my mother's face. "It appears to me that you would have mentioned this name Renee something right off if it was your real name, instead of saying Randy whatever you said. You got any relatives around here that could vouch for you?" He turned to me. "You got a grandmama or granddaddy anywhere, honey?"

My mother's eyes were burning into me, and I told the truth. "My grandparents live in Tulsa."

"That's right officer, my parents. My father's name is Horace Miller and they live on East Eighty-third Street in Tulsa. I can give you their phone number. Just call them."

The sheriff opened his mouth, stuck out his tongue a little, then made a sort of sucking noise. "Judy," he said, "get me a toothpick, please. I got a piece of salad stuck in my teeth from what I ate in here earlier. I can't think with something wedged in my teeth that way."

The woman smiled, and I was pretty sure she wanted to say that the sheriff couldn't think anyway, but she didn't and instead just took a little jar full of toothpicks from beside the cash register and held it out to him.

The sheriff was still holding the gun, but he shoved it out toward the woman. "You guard her, Judy," he said. "I got to get that lettuce. Now, don't take your eye off her, you hear me?"

"She won't escape from me," said the woman, and I thought she was about to laugh.

The three older ladies were getting up from their booth and moving toward the door. "We'll pay you next time, Judy," one of them called.

"Yes," said one of the others. "You seem to be busy apprehending dangerous criminals right now."

Sheriff Walters whirled around toward them. "Hold your horses," he yelled. "Nobody goes anywhere till I say so. I might need statements from you."

"For Pete's sake, Clyde Walters. Can't you see that this girl looks exactly like her mother? Call the grandparents if you have to, but we aren't staying," said one of them. They all three walked out.

"Ought to haul them all in," the sheriff muttered, then turned to Rendi. "Look here, lady," he said, "seems to me if you got married and had this little girl here that you claim is named Sparrow Miller, your parents wouldn't have the name Miller." He gave his head a satisfied nod to emphasize how smart he was to be finding a hole in Rendi's story.

"Robin. Her name is Robin, not Sparrow. After my husband deserted us, I had his parental rights terminated, and I had both of our names changed to Miller, my maiden name. I had her birth certificate amended too. The information is certainly on file. She was born in Tulsa, Oklahoma."

"Got it," the sheriff said, and I thought for a minute he meant he understood what Rendi was saying, but then he pulled out the toothpick with a piece of something green on it. He handed the toothpick to the waitress. "Throw this away for me, Angie," he said, and he took the gun away from the woman named Judy.

"Sheriff," said my mother, "will you please call my parents?"

He sighed again. "You say his name is Horse Miller?

• • • • •

42

Horse, is that his real name or is he some kind of hippie artist that goes around writing a made-up name on things too?"

"My father's name is Horace," said Rendi, "not Horse, and I can assure you that he is neither a hippie nor an artist. He is a bank president, First National Bank of Tulsa."

"Uh-huh," said Sheriff Walters, but there was doubt dripping from his voice. "Well, let's just take a little ride down to the station and see if we can get this all straightened out." He used his gun to motion toward the door. I started to worry that he might shoot Rendi accidentally. Wow! Wouldn't I feel guilty then?

Judy must have been thinking the same thing about the danger because she followed us out. "Clyde," she said when we were on the sidewalk, "I'm afraid for you to try to hold that gun and fasten the prisoner in her seat at the same time. Let's just leave your patrol car here and walk to the station. It would be safer."

"Don't need you putting in telling me how to handle dangerous criminals. I've taken in many a felon in my time."

"Rendi," I said when we were outside, "shouldn't I get the birth certificate? Where is it?"

"See," the sheriff yelled. "There's my proof. Children don't go around calling their mothers by their first names."

"Maybe not in Prairie Dog Town, Oklahoma," I said, "but I've been calling her Rendi all my life."

"Don't get smart with me, bird girl." He shot me a dirty look.

• • • • •

Rendi told me to look in a small box marked "Papers," and she told me to get the key out of her jeans pocket.

The sheriff told Judy to keep a close eye on me. Next he turned to Rendi, "Get hoofing," he said, and he poked the gun up close to her ribs. I didn't want to watch, so I turned toward the van. Judy followed me.

I had the door open when she caught up with me and reached out to put her hand on my arm. "She really is your mother, isn't she?" I nodded. "Why did you write all that business about being kidnapped?"

My face turned red. "I told the truth about being mad," I said.

This time Judy nodded. "I was a teenage girl myself once. It was a long time ago, but I can still remember how it was, got mad at my mama a time or two myself."

I looked at the woman closely for the first time. She was older than my mother, quite a bit older. Her eyes were brown, and so was her lined face, and I thought that Judy must have spent a lot of time in the sun, something my mother was always worrying about me doing. Judy looked kind, though. "Could you come to the police station with us?" I asked, because I was getting worried that Rendi might really get locked up. I was mad at her, but not mad enough not to care too much if she spent time in jail.

"Sure, honey," she said. "Angie can run the place while I'm gone, does it all the time, but don't you worry. Clyde will finally believe you. If I have to, I'll promise to drive over to Ponca City with him on his day off and go to a movie to get him to let your mother go." She gave me a little smile. "We tease Clyde, call him Barney Fife, you know, the dumb deputy on the old *Andy Griffith Show*. You ever watch that one on Nick at Nite?" I shook my head, and she went on. "Well Barney was a character. Truth is Clyde does remind me of him, and see, Clyde was a deputy for ages, always taking orders until old Sheriff Ward died three months ago. Being the real sheriff and carrying the gun is going to his head. Sheriff never let him carry a gun. On that TV program, Barney got in lots of messes like Clyde arresting your mother. Still, Barney had a good heart, and Clyde does too. He's been sweet on me since we were in high school, outlived two other men I married, just waiting for me to pay attention to him. Sometimes I go out with him."

Judy and Clyde, romance at their age! I was amazed, but I didn't stop moving boxes around so I could read the labels on them. Finally I found two small boxes jammed between the second seat and the van wall. One of them was marked pictures, but the other one said "Papers." I pulled it out and rummaged through it until I came to my birth certificates. It seemed strange, looking at the first one and seeing my name as being Robin Diane Douglas and Rendi's written as Renee Dee Douglas. I knew that had been my last name, but I had never seen it written out that way. I didn't have time to think about it, though,

* * * * *

45

because Sheriff Walters was marching my mother off to jail. I stepped over the boxes, climbed out of the van, and started after the sheriff and his prisoner.

After just a few feet, we turned a corner, and I saw a street I hadn't seen before. There were about six other buildings there, and one of them had a sign that read, "Sheriff's Office."

Inside, Sheriff Walters took the seat behind the desk. "I do my best thinking here in my sheriff chair," he said. I spread my birth certificates on the desk in front of him. Rendi told me to get her driver's license from the purse that hung on her shoulder. I got her billfold, took out the license, and several pictures to show Sheriff Walters. There I was, a curly-haired girl of about three sitting on Rendi's lap. Another picture was of us both when I was about seven, and there was my school picture from this year.

"See, Sheriff Walters, Rendi and I have always been together." He held up the pictures one by one, looking from the Rendi on paper to the Rendi standing in front of him with her hands in cuffs.

"Well," he said. "It does appear you're her mother. I'll need to make a couple of phone calls, one to the grandfather and one to the folks up in Denver. You might be the girl's mother, but not have custody of her or some such. Things like that happen nowadays."

"They do," said Judy, "and you are very smart to be on top of it all." I knew Judy was softening him up in case she had to persuade him to let Rendi go."

"I'll start with your daddy," he said to Rendi. "What'd you say the name of that bank is in Tulsa?" Then he looked at his watch. "It's two-thirty. Reckon, he'd still be there, banker's hours and all?"

Rendi repeated the name of the bank and added, "If my father isn't there, ask to speak to the vice president. His name is Ronald Johnson. He can tell you that I am Horace Miller's daughter and that I have a daughter named Robin."

The sheriff got the number and asked to speak to "Horse Miller," but whoever answered must have understood who he wanted because in just a minute I could tell he was speaking to my grandfather, asking all the questions about his daughter. When he put down the phone, he nodded his head slowly. "Well," he said, "I got to the bottom of this mystery. Mr. Miller says he has a daughter named Renee who folks call Rendi and a granddaughter named Robin. Said you lived in Denver, last he heard. He swore you have full custody and told the same story you did about the little girl's father. Didn't know a thing about you being in Oklahoma, though, but he told me he hoped you were coming to his house. I could tell you don't see each other no great lot. Ought to put you in a cell for not having more to do with your daddy and mama, but I don't know as there's a law against such. Reckon I'll have to let you go." He stood up, took a key from his pocket, went to my mother, and tried to open the handcuffs.

Judy stepped over to him. "Here, Clyde," she said, and she took the key from him. "Let me do this. You've got more important things to do." She had Rendi's hands free in a second and dropped the key on the desk.

"Here," said the sheriff, and he handed me back my yellow pad. "Don't suppose I'll need this for evidence." He shook his finger at me. "You ought to have a good talking to over writing down things that aren't true."

"Let's let this lady take care of her daughter, Clyde," said Judy, and she smiled at us. "I live in a duplex, rent out the other side, furnished. Are you two looking for a place to live around here?"

"Thank you," said Rendi, "but, no, I don't think Prairie Dog Town is right for us. We didn't get off to a very good start here, and probably we do need a place with a few more people."

"I want to go back to Denver," I said quickly. I thought maybe Rendi had already had enough of Oklahoma and had begun to see we belonged in the Mile-High City. "We had good times back in Denver, didn't we, Rendi?"

She nodded her head, but what she said was, "We did, but, Bird, we aren't going back there. You need to give up the idea. We'll find a place we both like." She took my arm and began to lead me to the door

I was angry again. I stopped walking. "If we can't go back home," I said, "we might as well live in Prairie Dog Town as anywhere else."

I expected Rendi to say no. I was only trying to be diffi-cult because I certainly had no desire to live in this place that was little more than a wide spot in the road, but to my surprise, Rendi said. "Okay, Judy, when can we see the duplex?"

That's how we came to live on Shade Tree Lane in Prairie Dog Town, Oklahoma.

Chapter 3

Rendi's brush with the law took place on Friday. We spent the rest of that day unloading our van, buying groceries, and driving by schools. I was surprised because I had thought Prairie Dog Town would have a little white building with a bell outside, like the one-room schools you see on old western movies on TV.

Actually, they turned out to have three separate buildings. The high school, on one side of town, was the newest building of the three, and there was a smaller building there that said, "Office of the Superintendent." I didn't look too carefully at the high school because I would be long gone before I finished my eighth-grade year. I had to believe that. The elementary school looked fairly new too, and it was on the other side of town from the high school.

My school was in the middle, just a block from the duplex we had rented. It was a big building made from a sort of red stone, and it was very, very old. A sign in front said, "Thomas Jefferson Middle School, Home of the Prairie Dogs." I was shocked. I threw my hands in the air. "I can't go there." I turned to Rendi: "You know you've always hated Thomas Jefferson."

She seemed surprised to hear me say such a thing. "Bird, Thomas Jefferson wrote the Declaration of Independence. How could I hate him? I don't like that he had slaves or what he did to one of the girls he believed he owned, but he was a product of his times. He wasn't as bad as the senator from one of the Southern states who fought against segregation even though he had a secret child with a black woman. It won't hurt you to go to Thomas Jefferson Middle School. Maybe you will learn a little history if you aren't busy sending notes to the Six-Pack."

"That building looks like it might have been where Thomas Jefferson went to school," I said.

On Saturday we finished putting our things away by noon. Rendi was totally happy about living in the place. I mean I could see why she liked the big sunroom that went all the way across the two duplexes. Judy told her right off that she could use it all for her studio, and she took her few belongings out of it. From the sunroom you could see a pasture that had a pond and cows. "Oh," said Rendi, "I've missed cows." She put her arms around me and gave me a little squeeze. "Don't they look beautiful against the sunset?"

No way would I say so, but I understood why she liked being able to see the sunset so well. That's something you couldn't do with big buildings and mountains all around you, but cows! "PUH-LEEZE, mother," I said. I had decided to stop calling her Rendi. I was too mad at her to want it to sound like we were friends. "I don't believe anyone could ever say cows are beautiful."

Rendi just laughed. "You might learn a thing or two in Oklahoma," she said.

After we finished unpacking, Rendi decided we should go back over to the town called Ponca City. Judy's place had some dishes and pots and pans, but Rendi wanted to pick up several household items. "You need school clothes too," she said.

She sang the song "Oklahoma" most of the way to Ponca City. I could see that being in her home state meant something to Rendi, and I kind of started feeling soft toward her. When she got to the part that said, "when the wind comes sweeping down the plain," I opened my mouth to join the song, but I caught myself. Remember you're mad at her, I told myself.

Ponca City was certainly bigger than Prairie Dog Town. I mean any place would almost have to be, but still I couldn't see how they got away with calling themselves a city. I hoped we would visit the *Pioneer Woman* again, but not wanting to sound interested in anything, I didn't say so. We went to Big-Mart, and Rendi picked up a few things, including a juicer to make our fresh orange and carrot juice.

We had a juicer in Denver, but Rendi said it was old, and she hadn't bothered to pack it. "That seems wasteful to me," I said, and I hoped I reminded her of Grandma. When we were headed toward the checkout, I asked, "Do you want me to buy my school clothes here?"

"Here?" Rendi was shocked because in Denver I was so-o-o particular about where I bought my clothes and would only consider one or two little boutiques and a few trendy stores in the mall, places where the rest of the Six-Pack shopped. "As we were driving in, I saw a little shop that looked cute. Don't you want to check it out?"

I shook my head. This was good. Rendi was definitely beginning to see that she had pushed me too far. "No," I said, "this will do fine. What do you want me to wear to school?"

She looked like I had slapped her in the face or something. "Bird," she said softly, "I am not suddenly going to start telling you what to wear. I just didn't want you to bring those lime green or orange pants, reminders of being just like a certain group. I want you to truly think for yourself. That's all."

"Good," I said, "I'll do just that." I moved through the jeans and other things girls might be wearing to school and headed toward a rack of ladies suits. "Size eight ought to fit," I said, and I took a navy blue skirt and jacket from the rack. I handed them to Rendi, then I took the same skirt and jacket in dark green, black, gray, and dark red. I piled the suits onto the top of the other things in our basket. "There," I said, "five outfits. That's all I need for five days of school."

"Bird!" Rendi was starting to sound more angry than guilty. "This is ridiculous. If I pay for these things, you are going to have to wear them. Do you understand me?" She was still holding the navy skirt and jacket. Then she whirled around and started hanging them back on the rack.

"So you won't buy these for me?" I folded my arms and stared at her.

"You're trying to do what I used to hear my mother call cutting off your nose to spite your own face. You're trying to hurt me, but you will only end up hurting yourself. Let's go look at some jeans or even go to another store." She reached for the other suits in the basket, but I put out my hand to stop her.

"I want the five suits," I said, and I took the navy outfit from the rack again, piled it on the top, and started to push the basket.

"Fine, but you are going to get very tired of wearing those things to school, very, very tired." She stomped after me.

"You must really like this suit," the lady who checked us out said to my mother as she folded the clothes to put them into bags. Then she looked at the size, and asked, "or are these for you?"

"No," said my mother in a sort of too-sweet tone. "Actually, I wouldn't be caught dead in them." She glanced at me and smiled a false smile. "These are for my daughter. Her taste in clothing seems to have changed lately."

I didn't say anything, but I stood my ground and glared right into Rendi's eyes. I would wear those things to school every day I had to go to Thomas Jefferson Middle School. I would wear them until my "hang loose" artist mother fell to her knees and begged me to forgive her. I would wear them until we loaded our van and went home to Denver, home to the Six-Pack.

The woman who checked us out put the bags of clothing in the cart with the other things we had bought, and Rendi started to push it out of the store to our van. I stopped her, though, and gathered up the three bags my suits were in. "I want to carry my clothes," I said, just like I used to want to carry the bags that had toys in them when Rendi bought me something while we were shopping.

She just looked at me, sighed, and shook her head. "Those things are probably too long for you," she said as we left the store.

"Remember I am tall. Besides, I like long skirts," I told her, and I marched out to the van. On the drive back to Prairie Dog Town, Rendi did not sing, and neither one of us said a word. We drove by the *Pioneer Woman,* but neither of us looked or said anything about her. I sat back in my seat and thought about how good my purchases made me feel. Not only had I made it plain to Rendi how she had destroyed my life, those clothes would make my life easier at my new school.

It was October; groups had already been formed in any class of eighth-graders. I sighed. The truth was that in a middle school in a place the size of Prairie Dog Town, the groups had probably been formed since kindergarten.

The kids at Thomas Jefferson Middle School were sure to think I was a weirdo when I showed up in a long suit like their grandmother might wear (my own grandmother wouldn't be seen in such things). It would be easier that way, easier to be rejected because of the way I dressed than just because no one wanted me around. I dreaded the thought of the first day at the new school less now. I would walk down the hall, and they would all stare at me openly. It would be better this way.

Rendi had made arrangements on Friday for our Internet connection, but they had told her it would probably be Monday before we could get online. We were surprised when we got home Saturday to learn that Judy had let the workers in, and our phone and Internet had been connected while we were gone. I spent all the rest of that day and most of the next writing long e-mails to my friends about how Rendi had almost gone to jail and about my

* * * * *

choice of clothing. I could hardly wait for them to write back to me.

The computer was on a desk in the living room. On Sunday afternoon, I saw Sheriff Walters drive up and park in front. For a minute, I thought he had come to check on us, but he went into Judy's side of the duplex. Pretty soon I saw them both go out and get in his car. I guess they both had Sunday off and were going out for a hot date or something. I waved to them. Judy was such a nice woman, and I was beginning to have a warm spot in my heart for the sheriff too. I mean, what if I had really been kidnapped?

On Monday morning I was up early. I pulled back my hair and tied it loosely with a black scarf. Then I put on the navy suit and a pair of black flats that I had hardly ever worn. There was a long mirror on the back of the door in my room. I stood in front of it staring at myself. I didn't even look familiar. I took a tube of lip gloss from my bag and put on just a bit. For a minute I considered taking off the suit and begging Rendi to take me to return those five outfits. I could buy some other things and start school the next day. Finally I got my courage back. "You look wicked," I said aloud. I was certain that Rendi would be ashamed of my appearance and know she had ruined my life.

"Good morning, Mother," I said when I came into the kitchen. She was eating cereal at the little table beside the window. An empty bowl with a spoon sat on the other side of the table along with a box of my favorite cereal and a jug of milk.

"Good morning, Daughter," Rendi said. She smiled, pleased that she had come up with a good reply. "Would you like some orange juice?"

"No, thank you, Mother," I said. "In fact, I don't want anything for breakfast." I twirled about slowly. "How do I look?"

"Very nice," she lied, and she stood up. "If you're sure you don't want to eat, we can leave now for your school."

"No!" I shook my head. I hadn't thought about Rendi going with me, but, of course, she would plan to go enroll me. I desperately wanted to go alone. I was afraid of what would happen if Rendi went with me. I was afraid I would break down when she got ready to leave. I was afraid I would cry like a kindergarten child whose mother leaves her for the first time.

"Bird, there will probably be something that I need to sign. I know you're mad at me, but the school is still going to want to see me. They will want to know there is really an adult involved, that you're not a runaway living under a bridge or something." She walked to the fridge to put away the milk.

"You can go tomorrow. I'll tell them you will sign stuff tomorrow. Please, Rendi. This is very important to me."

I guess my going back to her name convinced her because she said, "Okay."

I didn't go straight to school. I walked around, going a long way out of my way. I wanted to get to school after the first bell had rung. See, the thing was I wanted to walk down that hallway for the first time when it was empty instead of being full of strange eyes.

Until I got hit in the face with the date, I was kind of enjoying the pretty morning, but then I realized it was October 31, Halloween! Tonight my friends would be having a party without me. I considered just walking off. Maybe if I got back to the interstate, I could get a ride to Denver. Of course, I knew I would be too scared to do that. At least, I wasn't likely to get murdered at Thomas Jefferson Middle School.

I kept looking at my watch, and finally it seemed safe to head for the school. A ramp for wheelchairs went up one side of the wide stone porch, and there were big steps going up the front. On the first step, I stopped, drew in a deep breath, and imagined what stage directions Miss Deirdre would give me right now. I could almost hear her voice saying, "Hold your head high, Bird. Go into that big building and fill it up with who you are. Enter as if you were in charge." I straightened my shoulders and climbed the steps.

Just as I had hoped, there weren't any other kids going into the building. Everything looked pretty quiet. I would never admit it to Rendi, but I liked the feel of the old building. There were these neat old wood floors that were polished and shiny. I liked the smells too, old wood and polish, and something that made me think of all the kids who must have gone to school in the place.

On the doorway I had seen a sign saying, "All Visitors Must Report to the Office." Well, I was ready to report. The office was just inside the building. From halfway up the walls were all glass, so I could see into it from the hall. A long counter separated the room into two parts. The first part was small and it had a few chairs. Most of the office was behind the counter. A lady sat at a desk with a computer on it. Behind her was a door that said "Principal" above it. I didn't see any offices for a vice principal or a counselor. Thomas Jefferson Middle School was probably too small to even have people for those jobs.

I pushed open the door, stepped into the office, and walked to the counter. When the door closed behind me, the woman glanced up from her computer. I thought she must be between Rendi and my grandmother in age, probably fifty-something. She looked like a person I wouldn't want to have mad at me, but when she noticed me, she smiled and said, "May I help you?"

"I'm Robin Miller," I said. I was about to add that I wanted to enroll, but the woman didn't give me the chance.

She jumped from her chair, and her smile got real wide. "Oh," she said, "we didn't expect you until Wednesday, but come in. We are so happy you are here. Let me show you your office."

I was so surprised that I didn't say anything or move a muscle. The woman went to the little swinging gate that made it possible for people to go in and out of the inner office. She held the gate open, "Come this way, Ms. Miller," she said. "I can't tell you how thrilled we are to have you. It's been so hard not having a principal since Mr. Lawrence got sick. I just don't know what we would have done, if you hadn't been available to fill in."

My mind raced. This woman thought I was some sort of substitute principal. Wasn't this wild? I opened my mouth to explain, but I seemed to hear Miss Deirdre's voice again. "What a marvelous role, Bird," she said. "Who would have thought you would find such a wonderful part to play in Prairie Dog Town, Oklahoma. Go for it, darling. You can do it!"

I moved to go through the little gate. Why not have some fun on my first day at Thomas Jefferson? When I was in the inner office, I put out my hand to the woman. "Tell me your name again," I said. "I was told, of course, but I am afraid I've forgotten." I smiled. "Truth is, I guess I'm a little nervous on my first day."

"Nancy," she said, and she squeezed my hand. "Nancy Simpson. Welcome to Jefferson Middle School." When she let go of my hand, she motioned for me to follow her into the office. "Of course, we expect Mr. Lawrence back after Christmas, but I took the pictures off his desk and some of the personal things off the wall, just put them in a box in the closet. I'll have it all back when he returns, but I thought you might have your own things."

"I do have," I said. "My mother is an artist, mostly a sculptor, but I have a painting or two she's done also. I'll bring them and a small bust of Shakespeare she did for me when I got my master's degree." Most of that was a lie, but I thought it sounded good. To my personal knowledge, Rendi has never done a painting, but I suppose she had to do them in college some, and, of course, there is Richard, the missing father figure. Maybe that's what made me say painting. That idea about W. Shakespeare came to me because Rendi had made a piece like that for one of her friends in Denver, who did get a master's degree.

"How lovely," said Ms. Simpson, "and now you're working on a dissertation for a doctorate, and you so young."

I faked a small laugh. "Oh, you're flattering me now. I'm not so young, although I will say I still get carded sometimes when I go into a nightclub. It's an irritation now, but my mother tells me that these days of looking so young go quickly."

Pretty good one, huh? I'd heard a friend of Rendi's make that very same speech once. I was starting to be really glad that I am what our school counselor calls an "auditory learner," which basically means that I remember what I hear. I thought when she told me about the auditory stuff that I would rather have a photographic memory, but maybe being able to repeat what I've heard is very useful for me, now that I had so suddenly become a school administrator.

Mrs. Simpson laughed. "Your mother is right. She certainly is. Well, I'll leave you alone to settle in. I'm sure you won't have peace for very long. The teachers have been saving some discipline problems for you to handle." She walked out of the office, then stepped back inside and said, "Don't you be nervous, dear. You have old Nancy Simpson to help you." Then she went out and closed the door behind her.

My knees had got all weak, and I sank into this big comfortable chair behind the desk. I put my face in my hands. What had I done? This was crazy! I couldn't keep this masquerade up for long. When had Ms. Simpson said they expected the real substitute principal? Wednesday! Yes, that was it. Two days. Could I last that long? Probably not, but maybe I could last until lunchtime. Being the principal would be better than sitting through two or three boring classes, wouldn't it?

I relaxed a little. Then another thought came to me. What would they do to me when they discovered I was an imposter? Would Sheriff Clyde Walters come and take me away in handcuffs? They wouldn't execute me. How bad could prison be? No worse than being in the eighth grade at a new school. I was pretty sure of that.

The phone rang, and I froze. Should I answer it? I would

have to, wouldn't I? My hand was shaking when I reached out for it, but suddenly it stopped ringing. There was a knock on the door, and Ms. Simpson opened it just enough to stick in her head. "Should I show you about the phone?" she asked.

I wanted to make some excuse for not answering the ring she had obviously heard, but I couldn't think of any. "Yes," I said. "That would be nice."

She came around to my side of the desk, reached for the phone, and pushed a button. "I'm sorry I didn't do that earlier. When that button is pushed, you don't hear the phone unless I have answered and am putting the caller through to you. When I do put through a call, you will hear a ring and this button will light up." She pointed to the second button. "You also have a direct line to Superintendent Morris. When the phone rings and the second button lights up red, it's the Soup's office calling. The third button will light up green when the call is from anyone in Mr. Lawson's office over at the high school. Mrs. Newton is the principal at the elementary school, and her button is the fourth one. It flashes orange. It's simple. When you want to call those places, you just push their button."

She reached for a pad and pencil lying on the desk. "Here let me write it down for you." She repeated as she wrote, "Button one, white, Nancy. Button two, red, the superintendent, Mr. Morris is his name. I call him the Soup, but not to his face. Button three, green, Mr. Lawson, high school. Button four, orange, Mrs. Newton, elementary school. To call any of those people you only have to push their button. Just keep the note handy until you learn." She put down the pad, then picked it up again. Beside elementary school, she wrote, "Deaf." "The woman is almost deaf, can't hear well at all on the phone, but let me tell you she is sharp. Those kids don't get by with a thing nor anyone else either. Mrs. Newton doesn't miss a trick."

Pray Mrs. Newton doesn't call or show up, I said to myself, but it wasn't the elementary principal who I had to worry about. Of all things it was Angie from the City Café, but I am getting things out of order again. Angie didn't come until lunchtime. Well, not long after I had the phone explained to me, it rang, and a light started to flash. I grabbed Mrs. Simpson's note. The red light meant a phone call from the superintendent. I picked up the phone. "Good morning, sir," I said in the most adult-sounding voice I could come up with.

Mr. Morris laughed. "Now don't start calling me sir. I'm feeling ancient enough already. You call me Kenneth, like I told you. Almost everyone does, you know. I'm sorry to say it doesn't look as if I am going to make it over to visit with you today or even tomorrow. Things are stacking up around here, you know, and I am about to leave for a two-day conference on school finance in the city. I'm glad we got to have lunch together last week, gave us a chance to get acquainted, you know. Well, how's it going?

* * * * *

Didn't you tell me you couldn't come until Wednesday? I was surprised when I heard from Nancy Simpson that you were here, you know."

The man liked to say, "you know," but I didn't have time to think about that. He was questioning why I had shown up today. An answer came to me. "I found I was able to make it a couple of days early, anxious to get on the job. That's all right, isn't it?"

"More than all right, it's good. A school can't get along well without a principal, you know. Lawrence has been out two weeks already. Discipline problems are stacking up, you know. I'm afraid we've got us a couple of teachers over there who can't control the kids very well. No, the truth is there are three. You'll find out right away who they are. They've no doubt been saving up their discipline problems to send to you. I'm certainly glad you've had so much training in the area of discipline, you know."

He paused, and I knew I was supposed to say something. "Well, troubled kids have always interested me a good deal," I said with all the maturity I could muster in my voice. "Actually, I've been closely involved with some."

"When I met you, I said to myself, this lady is young, but she has something special, you know. I feel certain you can handle the job."

"Thank you, Kenneth," I said. "I feel certain I'll never forget my first time as a principal even though it may be brief."

* * * * *

"Well, good. There's one more thing. It's Nancy Simpson, fine woman, mighty fine. She's efficient too, practically runs the school. Well, that's the problem. She can sometimes forget who's in charge around there. She'll help you, but don't let her get the idea you work for her. She'd take over if you let her, you know. Well, mighty glad to have you, you know, and I'll be over to visit with you on Wednesday."

I told him thank you and said good-bye after he did. Then I sat in my chair smiling. It appeared no one but the superintendent had actually met this substitute principal, this other Robin Miller. I might actually last longer than lunchtime.

This could be the most fun I've had in a long time. I wished there was someone to tell. There was the computer, but I didn't want to e-mail. I wanted to talk to someone now. I looked at the clock. Nine thirty. That would be eight thirty in Denver, and Katie would be almost to school. She'd have her cell with her, and I could call her on this school phone. I reached for the phone and dialed the familiar number. "Hello," I said when she answered, "what are you doing?"

"Nothing," she said. "Mom's driving me to school. It's so good to get to talk to you and everything. What are you doing?"

"Nothing," I said, and then I laughed. "Well, nothing except being the principal of Thomas Jefferson Middle School in Prairie Dog Town, Oklahoma."

• • • • •

Katie screamed, "What?"

I told her the whole story. She got excited, talking loud and laughing. "Shush," I said. "I don't want your mother to hear and know what is going on. She might call someone."

"Oh, Bird," Katie said, "that's such a wickedly funny story. I really want to see the movie about the new girl getting to be the principal." I knew then that Katie's mother had been listening. "I can't wait to tell Ivory."

"Turn your phone on after second hour. I'll call you then, if I'm not too busy with business. There's a lot of work to be done around here." I hung up. For a few minutes, I sat in my chair taking deep breaths. This was like a roller-coaster ride, lots of fun, but scary too. Really scary!

Chapter 4

I didn't have long to sit and breathe because the phone rang and the first button flashed a white light. That meant the secretary wanted me. Her name had gone completely out of my head, and I grabbed up the list, Nancy, Nancy Simpson. I cleared my throat and picked up the phone. "Yes?"

"I don't like to bother you," she said, "but I was wondering about an announcement. Shouldn't you make an announcement, telling everyone that you are here?"

"An announcement?"

"Yes, on the PA system."

"The PA system?" This was not going well.

"Yes, of course, the public address system."

"Oh, yes, the public address system, the thing you use to call kids to the office." I looked around. What did a public address system look like? My eyes fell on a box sitting on a stand in the corner behind my desk.

"Should I come in and show you how to use it?"

"That would be nice."

She came right away and did go to the box. "See these switches and the room numbers below them?"

I nodded.

"You flip the switch to the room you want. You can speak or just listen. There's a schedule in your top desk drawer to tell you what teacher is in each room during a certain period. Teachers can call us by flipping a switch in their rooms too, but those calls go first to me. I've got one of these boxes behind my desk too. I flip a switch to pass the call on to you if there is an emergency, like some kid has passed out or something. See this green button? Push it if you want to do an 'all call.'"

I felt like it might be the new principal who passed out. "What's an 'all call'?" I asked.

"When you want everyone to hear you, like the announcement you're about to make." I guess I looked kind of clueless because she went on. "You know the one introducing yourself to the students and faculty."

"Oh, yes," I said. "Yes, of course." I considered asking Mrs. Simpson for advice about what I should say, but I remembered Superintendent Morris's warning about not letting her take over my job. You're the principal here, Bird, I told myself. "Thank you, Mrs. Simpson," I said. "You may go now. I'll make my announcement soon."

Mrs. Simpson looked at me, one eyebrow raised like

she was sort of measuring me in her mind. I felt she did not approve of me, but she did leave the office.

I took a piece of paper from a drawer so I could write out what I would say, but Mrs. Simpson called me on the phone. "You might want to say something about expecting the kids to behave. In some classes they've acted up."

"I might want to say that," I said, "but I'll decide in a few minutes. Thank you for your suggestion, Mrs. Simpson," I said. I was glad she was on the phone because I wouldn't have wanted to say that to her face.

"Of course," she said, and her voice wasn't as friendly as before.

Pretty soon, I had my announcement all written. I read it over several times, practicing sounding like a principal. Then I pushed the green all-call button. "Students and faculty," I said. "It is my pleasure to tell you that I am your new principal. My name is Ms. Miller. By the way, *Ms.* is spelled *m-s,* and it means that I might or might not be married, no one knows." I thought about that for a second and realized it didn't sound right. "Well, of course, I know if I am married or not, but it doesn't really matter here at school, does it? Anyway, I am the principal for the rest of this semester. I am sure you all know that the word *principal* is spelled with a *p-a-l* at the end when it means the principal of a school and with a *p-l-e* when it means a standard or something. I am glad my kind of principal is spelled with a pal because I want to be your pal. I think

● ● ● ● ●

students deserve a real pal in the principal's office, and that is what you have here at Thomas Jefferson Middle School for as long as I am here, which won't be real long." I realized I hadn't written a closing, but now it seemed like I needed one. "Over and out," I said, and I flipped off the all-call button.

For a minute, I just sat at my desk and waited for my heart to stop beating so fast. This acting job was the hardest I'd ever had. The phone rang. It was Mrs. Simpson, and somehow I didn't imagine she was calling to say she loved the announcement.

"I hate to bother you." She was speaking softly, little more than a whisper. "Well, maybe I'd better just come in and talk to you."

"Yes," I said, "do that."

In just a second, the door opened. Mrs. Simpson stepped inside and mostly closed the door after her, but kept looking through the crack. "Like I said, I hate to put this on you so soon, but something has to be done about Serenity Blair."

My heart started to race again. This kid, this Serenity, was obviously sitting in the outer office. According to Mrs. Simpson, something had to be done about the kid, and I was expected to do it. I swallowed hard and straightened myself in the principal's chair. "Give me a little background," I said. "What is Serenity's problem?"

Mrs. Simpson let go a very long sigh. "How do I explain

this? First, she was sent down here by her math teacher, Mrs. Street. Serenity is a problem in all of her classes, but she wouldn't stand up and slap another girl except in Mrs. Street's class. The woman has no control, and of course the kids have been taking advantage of the fact that we've had no principal." She stopped and smiled at me. "Serenity did her slapping just before your announcement, so she didn't know you were here. No doubt she'll be sorry now."

I studied her expression. Was she putting me on? Did she think I'd fall on my face, and was she just waiting to see it happen? I was starting not to like this woman. "Well," I said slowly. "I'd like to think I'll be able to help some troubled young people. I don't so much want to punish as to be a guiding hand, firm, but kind."

This time Mrs. Simpson laughed out loud. "That's good. I can tell you Serenity Blair can certainly use a guiding hand. The kids torment her, and I am afraid she brings most of it on herself."

I was proud of myself for not groaning out loud. A Marcy Willis type was about to come into my office. Then suddenly, I changed my mind. Good! Wouldn't I have loved to have a go at Marcy? I certainly knew what her problem was. I'd never get to straighten out Marcy, but here was this Serenity kid just waiting for my guidance.

Mrs. Simpson interrupted my thoughts. "Should I send her in now?"

• • • • •

I leaned back in my principal's chair. "Yes," I said, "I'm ready for Marcy."

"Serenity," Mrs. Simpson corrected. "The child's name is Serenity, but she certainly is not serene."

"Oh, yes," I said. "Send in Serenity."

You won't believe this, but it's true. This girl actually looked like Marcy Willis! Oh, maybe her face didn't look so much like Marcy's. The actual truth is I guess I never really looked real close at Marcy's face, but there was a similarity between the two girls, and it jumped right out at me, the same mousy brown hair with no style whatsoever, the same slouchy walk, and sort of nothing clothes, some kind of worn-looking beige pants.

"The files are over there, Ms. Miller," said Mrs. Simpson, who had followed the girl into the office. "Should I get Serenity's for you?"

"Oh, the file," I said. I should have thought of the file myself. Principals and counselors really love files. They were always whipping out mine. "Certainly, I will want the file."

Mrs. Simpson opened a filing cabinet, took out a thick folder, put it on my desk, and went out, closing the door after her. I was thinking fast, trying to remember what counselors and principals had said to me. Questions! They usually started with a question. "Well, Serenity," I said. "Would you like to tell me why you slapped a girl in math class?"

"Aren't you going to tell me to sit down first?"

• • • • •

"Yes," I said. "Certainly, take a chair if you would be more comfortable." I waved in the direction of the chair across from my desk.

Serenity settled herself in the chair, hunched over. I waited for her to look up, but she didn't. Nothing but silence. Just be quiet, I told myself. I'd had that silent treatment used on me, and I remembered that it had worked, made me start to talk.

"They pick on me," she finally muttered. "They pick on me all the time." Her voice got louder on the second sentence. I remained quiet. "You can read all about it. I bet there's plenty about it in that stack of junk about me."

I looked down at the papers in her file, shifted to the form on the bottom, and read. The note had been written by Serenity's first grade teacher. "Serenity is a happy, bright child. She has a wonderful imagination." Well, something sure happened to her since.

I put the papers back into a stack. "I could spend lots of time reading about you," I said to the girl, "but I'd rather hear what you have to say. Why do other kids not like you?"

Serenity shrugged, but she didn't look up. "They're jealous I guess."

I laughed out loud, and that made Serenity finally look up at me. "Why would they be jealous of you?"

She shrugged again. "I don't know. Maybe they're not jealous. They pick on me. That's all." She bit at her fingernails.

• • • • •

I wanted to slap her. "Stop biting your nails!" I yelled. "Don't you know you can't let them see you biting your nails or even let them know that your nails have been bitten. You can't let them know that they get to you."

She stared at me, confused. "Huh?"

"The people who pick on you! Don't let them know you bite your nails."

The girl looked up at me and shrugged. "Whatever," was her only answer. I didn't even think about what she said. It was the look on her face that got me. Her eyes were big and brown, and I guess they could have been pretty except they weren't. Those eyes made me think about a dog that someone kicked every day.

I wished Serenity would look down again. I didn't want to see those eyes anymore. The really wild thing was how I kept seeing Marcy Willis, like she was the one sitting in that chair. Suddenly I could totally remember how Marcy looked, especially the way her eyes were. I did not want to see Marcy Willis in Prairie Dog Town, Oklahoma. I got up and walked over to the window. I'd finish the discussion without looking at Serenity, but I had to say something. I wanted the girl out of my office. "Who picks on you? The whole eighth grade? Do they all hate you?"

"I don't like to talk about this stuff," she said.

A strange feeling came over me. I whirled around and stomped my foot. "Well, you're going to talk about it," I yelled, "and I am going to put a stop to this nonsense."

That last part just sort of came out. What nonsense did I mean? I wasn't sure. I didn't even know whose side I was on, Serenity's or the girls who picked on her.

Serenity looked up, surprised, but she wasn't nearly as surprised as I was. Could I really think I wanted to help this girl? I went back to the desk and sat down behind it. "Now first you tell me who picks on you." I tore off the page of notes about the phone and shoved the empty pad across the desk. Then I held out the pen. "Here, I want a list."

"Are you going to punish them?" Serenity looked up at me, and her sad brown eyes got even bigger. I couldn't tell if she was hoping or afraid I would punish her tormenters. "Because if you give them detention or something, they will just take it out on me."

"Write," I demanded. "I want the name of every person who has ever picked on you. I'll get you more paper if you need it."

She started to write. After a while she stopped, looked over her list, and drew a line across it to separate some names. Then she pushed the paper across the desk to me. "That's most of them, I guess," she said. "The main ones anyway, the ones who make my life miserable." She sat back in her chair, folded her arms, and watched me.

I studied the list. There were four names, then a line followed by three more names. "What's the line for?" I asked.

"The first names," she began to count them off on her

fingers, "Nicole, Caitlyn, Katelin, pronounced the same, but with different spellings. They call themselves *C* and *K*. Anyway those three girls and Ashley, they are the most popular girls in our class. They treat me the worst. The others . . ." She paused, shrugged, and then went on, "I guess they want to be popular too. I guess they want to be in that group, and they think picking on me might get them in."

I didn't know what to say next, so I said, "Hmm," and leaned back in my chair. Then I remembered something. "Now tell me what you do to make them pick on you."

"Nothing," she said, and her tone was miserable. "Three of them have always been best friends, even in kindergarten, but back then mostly everyone used to get along. Back when we were little, I mean, sometimes, kids would be mean, but the next day we'd play together. Now Ashley is best friends with them too, and they . . . well, they think they're hot or something. That's all."

"And there aren't even six of them, are there?"

"No," she said, and she leaned toward me. "Why would you think that?" She didn't wait for me to answer, just went on. "They call themselves the Purples because they all four have purple jackets. They wear them even when it isn't cold, like today. You know how warm the weather is, but they came to school in those purple jackets. Makes me sick."

I was interested. "Even in kindergarten? They had little purple jackets even back then?"

"Nah, not back then." She sort of threw up her hands.

"Why do you need to know exactly when they got the stupid jackets? What difference does it make?"

"Well," I said, "I just think they could get a better name than the Purples. They could even call themselves the Four-Pack." I realized that didn't sound very principal-like, so I shuffled around the things in Serenity's file while I thought. Then I remembered. "But you do something to make them pick on you. Mrs. Simpson said so."

Serenity fell back in her chair and put her hands up to her face like I had slapped her. "She said that? Mrs. Simpson said I do something to make them tease me?"

"She did. Now tell me what you do?"

"I thought Mrs. Simpson was my friend," Serenity said. "I thought she liked me. She's always nice to me when I come into the office."

I was disgusted. Her whining voice made me think of Marcy Willis, and I did not want to think about that person. "I am not concerned here with what Mrs. Simpson thinks of you. As a matter of fact, she probably does like you, but she obviously knows why the Purples don't." I pounded my fists down on the desk hard. "I think you have some idea too. You look like a smart girl to me. Are you going to make me ask Mrs. Simpson to come in here and testify? That wouldn't be very pleasant for you, would it?"

Serenity shook her head and stared down at her sneakers. "I don't have nice clothes," she said. "The Purples all have nice clothes?"

"Really?" This subject really did interest me. "Where do they buy them? I didn't see many places to shop around here." Serenity rolled her eyes like she thought a principal wouldn't ask that. Focus here, Bird, I told myself. I sort of cleared my throat. "Well," I said. "Maybe it doesn't matter where they buy them. Let's get on with the matter at hand." I was proud of coming up with that phrase, "the matter at hand." Things I had heard in the principal's office were coming in handy for me now. "Does every girl who doesn't wear the latest fashions get picked on, then?"

Serenity gave me a surly look and shrugged her shoulders. "Serenity," I said, and I leaned toward her. "Do not shrug when I ask you a question. I expect words in your answer. Do you understand me?" I was surprised to hear how principalish I sounded. Well, the girl was getting on my last nerve. Shrugging seemed to be her number one talent. "Now, I want to know if every girl who does not dress in a certain way is tormented!"

"No," she said, "just me."

"Very well, then, I think we can eliminate your clothing as the reason. I suggest you look a bit more deeply." I looked at her and waited, taping my fingers against my desktop and humming the song "Oklahoma."

"Maybe it's partly the things I say." She was staring at the floor again.

"Give me an example." I tried to make my voice warm, yet firm.

"Sometimes I exaggerate things." I could barely hear

her, but as soon as the words sunk into my brain, I knew we were getting to the root of the problem.

"Serenity," I said. "I know this is hard for you, but I can only help you if you are honest with me. What things do you exaggerate? Give me an example."

Tears started to roll down her cheeks. "The other day in history class the kids got Coach Pickle to talking about movies. If we can get him off the subject of history, sometimes we don't have to do anything all period." She stopped talking then, like she was finished with the story.

"Come on, Serenity. What did you say?"

"Well, Coach Pickle started talking about this Marilyn Monroe woman and how he loved her old movies." She stopped again.

"Yes," I said, "I know about Marilyn Monroe." I started using my hand like I was urging her to move. "Come on. What did you say?"

"Well, I put up my hand and I was going to say that I had watched some of Marilyn Monroe's movies, but I didn't." She stopped talking and made little sobbing sounds instead.

"I'm waiting," I said, using my hands again.

"I sort of said that I was adopted and that Marilyn Monroe was my birth mother."

I laughed out loud, and Serenity stopped crying to say, "You're not supposed to laugh at me and stuff. You're supposed to make me feel better."

"Serenity," I said, "Marilyn Monroe died ages ago. My

• • • • •

mother told me once it was a long time before she was even born. Marilyn Monroe couldn't possibly be your birth mother."

"I didn't know when she died. I didn't even know she was dead." She wiped at her eyes with her hand, and I pulled a tissue from the box on my desk and handed it to her. Suddenly she stopped dabbing at her eyes. "Ms. Miller," she said, "how old are you?"

"Serenity, I don't think that my age is . . ." I paused. Trying to talk like a principal was suddenly hard. My mind raced. "Relevant! I mean my age is not relevant to this conversation."

She shrugged, and that was when I learned she was as good in math as she was in shrugging. "Well," she said, "I was just wondering because Coach Pickle said Marilyn Monroe died in 1962, and if that was before your mother was born, she must not be over forty-two, and that is pretty young for a principal's mother." She smiled at me.

"Did I say before my mother was born?" I didn't wait for her to answer, just went on fast. "Of course, I meant to say before I was born. Of course my mother would have to be lots older than forty."

"So," said Serenity, "you're over thirty, then?" She leaned across the desk to peer closely at me. "You look pretty good for that age."

This idiot girl was beginning to make me nervous. "Face cream," I said. "I use a lot of face cream." Then I remembered something important. "And stay out of the sun, Serenity." I nodded my head seriously. "Sun, that will make you look old before your time."

"Are you married, Ms. Miller?"

"Serenity, my personal life is not open for discussion, but I will tell you that I am not married. I have been too busy with my studies and my work to . . ." I sort of trailed off thinking what to say.

"To find a boyfriend? You've been too busy to find a boyfriend, right? Well, maybe I can help you out. Coach Pickle isn't married either. I think he was, but his wife left him or something. He's probably about your age."

"Serenity," I stood up. "Stop this nonsense at once. I would certainly never date a man who teaches at this school. It wouldn't look good to the school board or to Superintendent Morris."

"Sorry." She put up her hand as if to stop me from hitting her. "I didn't mean to set you off or anything. I guess you're pretty sensitive about not having any men in your life. I won't bring it up again."

I wanted to get the subject back to her, and I sat back down. "Tell me what happened in history class after Coach Pickle said Marilyn Monroe died in 1962."

"They all laughed, and today in math class, Nicole said right out loud that I was a big fat liar. Then I got up and slapped her."

"Well, you aren't fat, but I'd have to say you are a liar.

Why do you make up lies and tell them at school? You know people will not believe you."

Serenity pushed her lips together hard, and at first I didn't think she was going to answer, but finally she started talking. "I don't know. Usually I'm just sitting there kind of daydreaming. I don't have any plans to say anything out loud, but then I get to thinking it would be so neat if what I was daydreaming about turned out to be true, and the next thing I know, I've said my dream out loud."

I tapped my fingers against the desk again and tried to think of what to say. I was pretty sure there had to be more to Serenity's problem than just not being able to keep her mouth shut. I had heard enough from counselors and principals and during my "deep inside yourself talks" with Rendi to know that adults always wanted to talk about serious reasons for kids acting out. I couldn't come up with any reasons that Serenity made stuff up, and I was pretty sure she wasn't going to come up with any right now. I'd have to stall for time. "Tell you what, Serenity," I said. "Why don't we end our little talk for right now and continue tomorrow."

"What time?" she said, "I could miss English again." I thought she looked too hopeful, and I made myself a note to check her schedule and make sure she didn't miss English again. "I'll call for you," I said. That was something I knew plenty about, being called to the principal's office. Then I remembered the last conversation I had had with

Mrs. Howard, the counselor at my school in Denver. Like I told you, one of my real talents is remembering words. Anyway, I decided to repeat what Mrs. Howard had said to me, just with changes to make it fit Serenity's situation. "Before you go, though, I have a bit of wisdom to share with you." Mrs. Howard hadn't used that part about "wisdom," but personally I thought it was a good touch. "You know what the *Titanic* was, don't you, Serenity?"

"Sure," she said "I saw the movie, and we talked a bunch about it in Coach Pickle's class."

I wondered if she meant they had talked about the movie or about the real ship in Coach Pickle's class. I made a note that said, "Try to get into C. P.'s history class." I mean, I was the principal now, but I knew I would have to go to history class eventually. I got back to Serenity. "Good. Remember how the people fought over places in the lifeboats?" I waited for her to nod, and then I went on. "Well, Serenity, middle school is a lot like the *Titanic*. People who are in the right crowd, the in-group some people call it, well, those people aren't really bad people, but they are scared, just like the people on the *Titanic*. They get vicious when they're scared. They are afraid if other people get in the boat, or in the in-crowd, there won't be room for them, so they turn vicious and start hitting people over the heads with oars and stuff to keep them out of the boat."

Serenity stood up. "Well, Ms. Miller, I'll tell you. I am

tired of being hit over the head. I am just real real tired of it. Sometimes I think I'd be better off dead."

I looked up at her. The look in her eyes made me look away. This girl had a serious problem, and I wanted to help her, but even more than wishing I could figure out how to help Serenity, I wished I could go back to Denver. I wished I could turn back time. I wished I could refuse to put that note in the slot. No, I'd go even farther back than that, back to lunch the day before. If I could go back to the cafeteria that day, I would scoot over and ask Marcy to sit beside me, and I wouldn't even care what Ivory said about it either.

Chapter 5

When Serenity left, I just sat in my chair and thought about Marcy Willis. From where I sat now, Marcy looked totally different. From a principal's point of view, she seemed like a kid who needed help. Oh, sure, I had told Rendi that the Six-Pack had been trying to help Marcy, but it was a plain lie. I had felt a little bad for Marcy, but I didn't like to dwell on it.

"Is this seat taken?" she had asked that last day at lunch. The seat was beside me, and I had my bag on it to save it for Stephanie.

"Marcy," Ivory said from the other side of the table. "You know that seat is taken. You can count, can't you?" She paused, sort of cocked her head, lifted her eyebrows, and looked straight at Marcy. "Duh? One, two, three, four, five." She pointed at each of us as she counted. "Five of us here, so of course that seat is saved for our missing member."

"I just thought . . ." Marcy let her voice trail off.

I glanced across the table at Katie, and she was kind of biting at her lip. Katie and I didn't really care about Marcy, but what had happened with Marcy the week before when she wanted to sit with us in assembly made us feel sort of weird and embarrassed. Ivory had told her to quit trying to hang around us. Katie and I had talked about how we wished Ivory wouldn't be so mean sometimes, but, of course, we hadn't said anything to the others.

"Move on, Marcy," said Felicity that day in the lunchroom. "Like we told you before, we aren't looking to take any more girls into our group." She laughed, "I mean, we couldn't be the Six-Pack then, could we?"

Marcy looked like someone had slapped her. "Don't get excited. I don't want to be part of your silly group," she said. "I was just looking for a place to eat. You make me sick."

Marcy walked off, and Ivory hit the table with her hand. "Okay, that does it," she said. "It's time we taught that little twit a lesson."

"That's right," said Taylor. "She is really getting on my nerves."

Before the lunch period was over, we had a plan. We would type a note on a computer in the library and print it out. The wording was important. It would say, "Dear Evil Group, You have been mean to me for far too long. Now you will pay. My father has a gun, and I will bring it to school." We would sign it, "Marcy."

I knew it was wrong to write that note. I knew schools got really excited about guns. "Wait, guys," I said when Stephanie read back what we had settled on. "This is serious stuff we are messing with here. We could get in big trouble. I mean BIG."

"Why would we get in trouble?" Ivory shook her head. "No, it's whiny little Marcy who will be in trouble."

"She will tell them right off that we wrote the note," said Katie.

"So? How can anyone prove we did it? All we have to do is stick to the same story, right?" said Felicity.

"Let's take the pledge," said Ivory. "I promise to tell absolutely no one that we wrote a note. Pledge," she said, and she looked at each of us until we pledged.

"Hey," I said, relief flooding through my body. "If we use the library computer we will be listed on the sign-up sheet. They'll know right off."

"True," said Katie, and I could see that she was glad, "and it would be too risky to use a computer from any of our houses."

"Okay," said Ivory. "I've got it. There's this Internet café place across from where my mom works. I'm supposed to go down there after school today to wait for her so we can go shopping." She flipped her hair away from her collar. "I'll go to the computer place first."

"Great plan," said Felicity.

"Marcy will know we did it," I protested.

• • • • •

"Good," said Ivory. "Maybe it will teach the mouse a lesson!"

"Yeah!" Taylor rubbed her hands together, like she was dusting them off. "We won't be bothered with Marcy Willis anymore."

That night I couldn't eat any of the pizza Rendi ordered for us. I didn't want to talk to any of my friends on the phone either. I turned off my cell. "If anyone calls me tonight," I told Rendi, "tell them I went to bed with the flu."

"What's wrong?" she asked. I told her I had a problem, but I didn't feel like talking about it yet. I went to my room and thought about whether I had the nerve to quit the Six-Pack. If I did, I knew my former friends would hate me. They might even do something to me worse than they were doing to poor Marcy, and who would I run around with? I didn't want to walk down those halls alone all the time.

Finally, I did go to bed, telling myself that Marcy had brought it all on herself, and besides maybe Ivory would change her mind. Maybe she would come to school tomorrow and say the whole thing was off. She didn't, though.

I got to school late on purpose. There were only five minutes left before first hour when I got to my locker. I didn't care if I was late. I just wanted to avoid the Six-Pack, but they came while I was digging for my algebra book.

"Where have you been?" Ivory sounded a little angry.

"Had trouble getting Rendi up again," I lied.

"Well, we had a meeting without you, and you've been elected." Stephanie laughed.

Ivory held out her hand, and I saw the piece of folded white paper. "Here," she said, "take this into the library and put it in the book drop. Hurry."

"Someone might see me."

"So what? Don't you have a book to drop in? You most always do," Felicity said.

"I don't have one this morning." My stomach was starting to hurt. I looked at Katie, but she was staring at the floor.

"You'll think of something to do there," said Taylor.

"We'll all walk down there with you, but hurry. If we're late, it will call attention to us," said Ivory, and we started to walk.

My legs felt heavy, but I kept moving. Taylor got to the library first. Her hand shot out to open the door, and she held it for me. "After you," she said.

I didn't think I could move, but I did. Mrs. Evans was standing right by the spot at the counter where the book drop was. She looked up from her work and smiled at me. She had a book in her hand about Abraham Lincoln being killed. I had been wanting to read it because part of it is told from the viewpoint of John Wilkes Booth. I knew I was on the waiting list, but I started to talk to her about it anyway. "Oh," I said, "is it my turn yet?"

"No," she said, and she smiled at me. "There is still one person ahead of you." Just then a fight broke out between two boys over by the door. Mrs. Evans rushed over there yelling, "Stop that at once."

I figured no one was watching me, but I was still careful. I put my hand on the edge of the counter, moved up close so no one could see, and bent over to drop the note in the slot.

"Get to class everyone," Mrs. Evans said, and she went out the door, a hand on each boy's arm. I didn't know that Ivory had taken the book until we were outside of the library. "It's your reward," she said, and then she said that part about how I'd have it read in no time.

"Good job," I heard her say before we separated, but I couldn't say anything, not a word.

Marcy was in first period class with me. When Mrs. Golliver gave our assignment, I sat in my chair writing numbers on my paper. They weren't the right numbers. I didn't even try to copy the problems correctly. My stomach hurt really bad. It wasn't long before the voice from the office said, "Mrs. Golliver, will you send Marcy Willis to the office please?

Marcy passed my desk on her way out. I kept my eyes on my paper. I remember how I thought I would have to do the algebra assignment all at home that evening, but of course, that didn't happen. That was one algebra assignment I never had to do at all because before the day was over Rendi had checked me out of that school for good.

It wasn't thirty minutes before that same voice on the PA system called for me. That walk to the principal's office seemed so long. My friends were already in the outer office when I came in. Katie looked scared. I couldn't tell about Felicity, Taylor, or Stephanie, but there was no doubt about the look on Ivory's face. She met my gaze and shot me one of her, "Don't you dare fail me" messages with her eyes.

I didn't fail her. They made us go into the office one by one and face questioning. Mr. Kaylor, the principal, and Mrs. Howard, the counselor, played "good cop, bad cop," with us. Mr. Kaylor walked around his office. "Come on, Robin," he yelled, "tell us the truth. We know you girls wrote that note."

"I don't know what note you're talking about," I said.

Mrs. Howard sat at the end of Mr. Kaylor's desk. She leaned over to touch my arm. "Robin, I've always thought you were a good-hearted girl. I can't believe you liked doing something like this to another person."

I could feel my lower lip start to quiver, but I swallowed back the tears. "I don't know what you mean."

Mr. Kaylor called all our parents, and we had to sit outside the office while he talked to them. The door was closed, but Ivory's mother's voice came right through. She was yelling about how the school had no right to punish us if there was no proof we were guilty. I couldn't hear Rendi saying anything, but I knew by the way she had looked at me when we were all in there together that she knew I was guilty.

Now, sitting in the principal's chair in Prairie Dog Town, Oklahoma, I started wanting to talk to my mother. Rendi had written our new phone number on a piece of paper that she stuck in my skirt pocket just before I left. "In case you need me to enroll or something," she had said. I took out the number and called it. "Hello," she said.

For a second, I couldn't say anything, and I was afraid she might hang up. She didn't though. She knew somehow that it was me, and we didn't have caller ID on our new phone. "Bird," she said. "Is that you? Are you okay, honey?"

I found my voice then. "I'm okay. I just . . . well, I wanted to say I'm sorry for disappointing you. I mean with the Marcy thing. It was really bad for us to treat her that way."

"You're right, Bird, and I am proud of you for admitting it. Maybe one of these days you will want to write Marcy or call her. I think she should hear that you're sorry."

"Maybe so," I said. "I've got to go. I'm using the principal's phone, and I can't talk long. They don't give me any time to waste around here."

I heard her say, "Good," before I hung up.

I looked at the list of names Serenity had given me.

Should I call in the Purples? Nicole, Katelin, Caitlyn, and Ashley. She had not used last names. I guess in the eighth grade at this little school last names were not a thing you needed to use a bunch. I took the list out to Mrs. Simpson and asked her to have the girls sent to my office.

"Oh, the Purples." She took off her glasses, leaned toward me, and whispered. "I'd advise you not to see them all at once."

Mrs. Simpson and her advice were beginning to get on my nerves. After all, I was supposed to be running this place. I didn't protest, though. "We'll start with Nicole, then," I said. I turned to go back into my office.

"Wait," said Mrs. Simpson. "It might help if you know something about Nicole. She used to be a sweet little girl. The family lives next door to me. Well, two years ago her mother met some man on the Internet, left her husband and three kids for him. She lives out in California, they say. I don't think the child has seen her mother since."

"I see," I said.

I left my door open until Nicole came. "Come in," I said when I saw her in the doorway. "Close the door, please, and have a seat." I pointed toward the chair across from my desk. For a minute, I just looked at her. She was pretty except that I could see she wore too much makeup. Her dark hair was thick and curly, and her neck was the perfect length. She had on a totally awesome black outfit, but she looked scared.

"Am I in trouble?"

I leaned way back in my chair. "Why would you think that?"

She shrugged her shoulders. "Well, I mean, why else would I be called down here?"

"I like your purple jacket," I said. "Do you wear it often?"

"Is this about Serenity Blair?"

"Serenity Blair?" I sort of twisted my face like I was thinking hard. "Oh, is she the girl who slapped someone this morning?"

Nicole tossed her curls. "I am the person she slapped."

"Ummm, any idea why she would do a thing like that?"

She rolled her eyes. "Who knows why Serenity does anything? She went off her nut, I guess."

"Hmmm."

"She's always making up wild stories and acting gooney."

"Hmmm."

"Well, she gets on everyone's nerves. I'm not the only one."

"I see," I said, "so, of course, her getting on your nerves gives you the right to be cruel to her. Is that correct?"

"Cruel? I'm not cruel."

"I hope not, Nicole. Not so long ago, I was young like you. I was cruel, Nicole, very cruel, and you know what? I can't go back and change that although I would like to do that."

* * * * *

She looked down and started to zip her purple jacket. "You may go now," I said. "It has been a pleasure to have this little talk with you."

She got up and hurried from my office.

* * * * *

Chapter 6

After Nicole left, I wanted to crawl under my desk and hide. I knew I could just walk out the front door, tell Rendi what had happened, and convince her to move on. I could tell her that I'd learned my lesson. I could promise her I would never tease anyone again, but I didn't want to do that. I wanted to help Serenity and even Nicole. I could see that Mrs. Howard was right. Middle school is a major *Titanic,* and lots of the passengers are scared. I knew it was crazy for me to think I could do anything about it, but I wanted to try.

I would have to do some real thinking about what to do, but right now I needed a break. Eleven. That would be ten in Denver, time for my TV show. During the summer I had gotten really interested in *Trading Places,* all about how people would trade houses or apartments and decorate them. Sometimes the real owners liked what had been done, but not always. All of the Six-Pack watched it. Sometimes Katie still watched a soap opera called *All My Secrets,* but she never told Ivory. We were talking about how we might get our parents to let us redo each other's rooms, but we hadn't asked yet.

Why not make the best of my time in this office? It would be relaxing to watch my show. I picked up the phone and pushed the secretary's button. "Mrs. Simpson," I said, "is there a TV I could have brought into this office?"

"There are a couple of TVs on rolling stands in the library. Do you want to have one brought in to you?"

"Yes, please see to that for me."

"Is something going on? I mean has something important happened somewhere that you need to stay up with?"

This woman was a bit too nosy for my taste. I wanted to put her in her place, let her know not to question the boss's every move, but I didn't know how to go about doing that. I had to come up with a reason for wanting a TV, and I had to do it pretty quick. "Weather," I said. "I'm concerned about the weather." Should I say snow?

Mrs. Simpson saved me. "Oh, are there tornado warnings? I thought it looked a little cloudy when I went out to pick up the mail."

Tornadoes! Of course, that was it. In Denver we might have snow in late October, but I was pretty sure that it was too early for that in Oklahoma. "Yes, I am concerned about tornadoes. We can't be too careful when it comes to our students' safety."

"Oh, certainly not! I'll have a TV set brought to you at once." She hung up the phone, and pretty soon there was a knock at the door.

"Come in," I said, and because I had been over at the window, checking the weather. I opened the door myself. A boy pulled a TV on a cart into my office.

At first his back was to me, so I didn't see his face. When the TV was inside, he turned to me. "Where do you want this thing?" he asked. "I'll plug it in for you."

My mouth dropped open, but not to answer him. For a minute I just stood there with my mouth gaping, and I stared at him. He was awesome. I am not putting you on. Here was the absolutely best-looking boy I had ever seen. His hair was a mixture of blond and light brown, and I thought it was probably sun bleached because his skin was golden too. His eyes were the color of seawater, sort of a mixture of green and blue. He was tall enough to make me look up at him, which doesn't happen with a lot of middle school boys because I'm five-seven. Rendi says most of the boys will be taller than I am by the time we are in tenth grade or so, but right now lots of them are still shrimps. He was strong-looking too, not all muscled up like a deformed weight lifter, but solid. He had to ask me again, "Where do you want this?"

● ● ● ● ●

I was completely dazed by him, and I had to give myself a little shake. "Over there," I pointed. "You can plug it in and face it toward my chair." I went to the chair and sort of fell back into it, my eyes glued to him. He plugged in the TV and started toward the door. I couldn't let him go so soon. Who could care about TV with him around? I had to keep this hottie in my office a little longer. "What's your name, young man?" I asked.

"Kash Edge," he said. He was so gorgeous, and I was so lost in looking at him that I almost forgot to say anything else.

He started toward the door, and I sort of came out of my spell. "Wait," I almost yelled. "I mean, you aren't in any hurry to get back to class are you?"

"I was in the library working on a research paper about global warming."

"Oh, global warming! I love global warming!"

"You do?" His voice sounded surprised, and I figured global warming wasn't something people were supposed to love.

"I meant to say I'd love to know more about global warming." I waved at the chair across the desk from me. "Sit down and tell me. What is global warming?"

Kash did not look comfortable, but he sat down. "Don't you know what global warming is?" he said. "I mean, you're the principal, and it's on the news and everything."

I nodded slowly while I thought what to say next.

"Well, certainly, I know what other people are saying about it, but I'd like to hear what Kash Edge thinks."

"I'm just getting started on my paper, but I think we'd better do something about it."

"My opinion exactly." I reached for my pad of paper. "In fact, I'm making myself a note to bring up global warming at the next faculty meeting. I think I'll appoint Coach Pickle as head of the global warming committee."

Kash looked doubtful. "Well," he said, "I guess that's a good idea."

I leaned across my desk, so I could get a closer look at Kash. "Is everyone in your class doing a research paper?" I asked.

"Everyone in the eighth grade is doing one for English class," he said.

"I see, and what is your girlfriend writing about?"

Kash grinned. It was a just a little smile, but it gave me the idea of what his face would look like with a big smile. His teeth were white and perfect, no braces. I wasn't surprised. Greek gods most generally do not wear braces. "I don't have a girlfriend," he said. "Well, not anymore at least. I just broke up with her." He shook his head slightly. "She wanted me to call her on the phone. I mean every night. I've got things to do. Besides homework there's ball practice, and lots of times I help down at my dad's grocery store carrying out groceries and stuff."

"It does seem unreasonable to expect such a busy young man to make a lot of phone calls," I said, and I tried to make my voice sympathetic. "I see why you have such a strong-looking body, being an athlete and carrying groceries and all."

"I guess so." He glanced at the door.

I looked at my watch. It was time to call Katie, and besides I knew he wanted to leave. "Kash," I said. "You may go now, but I'll probably be calling you back into my office soon. I am trying to get to know the students here at Thomas Jefferson better, and I think you are the perfect one to start with."

"Thank you, Ms. Miller," he said. I opened my mouth to tell him to call me Bird. I stopped myself just in time. Instead I said, "I hope we are going to be friends, Kash, very good friends, indeed."

When he was out the door, I grabbed the phone to call Katie. She answered right off. "What are you doing? Don't say nothing. Tell me everything, and talk fast. The break is almost over."

"Sorry. I couldn't call earlier because the hottest boy in the world was in my office. He goes to school right here, and he doesn't have a girlfriend."

"What does he look like? What's his name."

"His name is Kash Edge. Don't you think that sounds like a movie star or something? He's got this sun-bleached hair and a golden tan. He's tall and you should see his body. I'm calling him back into my office this afternoon. I told him I want to get to know the students."

"What are you going to talk about?"

"I don't know. Any ideas?"

"Ivory just told me that she called the Psychic Emergency Line last night to find out who we should ask to take your place with the Six-Pack. She gave me the number and wants me to call tonight and see if we get the same advice. I didn't tell her, but I can't call. My father would kill me. It's real expensive."

"Give me the number," I said.

Katie told me the number, and I scribbled it on the principal pad. Just before we hung up, she asked a favor. "Bird," she said, "would you ask who should be the new girl in the Six-Pack? We're considering Beth Jones and Emily Cummings. Last night the psychic suggested Beth. I don't want Ivory to be mad at me."

I wasn't crazy about seeking advice on who my replacement should be, but I did understand why Katie didn't want Ivory upset. I told her I would ask.

I looked at the clock. It was twenty-five minutes after eleven. If I wanted to see much of *Trading Places,* I would have to turn on the TV now, but I was also really anxious to call the Psychic Emergency Line. Well, I had watched TV and talked on the phone at the same time before. I rolled my chair over to the TV, got the remote, and switched it on. I flipped through the channels; only four of them. The school didn't have cable! Maybe it wasn't even available here in the wilderness!

I left the TV on Katie's show, *All My Secrets*. Katie had told me some about it, and I caught on to what was going on pretty quick. A character named Lila had just returned from a terrible bout with amnesia that made her walk off and get lost just before her wedding. Her return was very interesting because Jeff, the man she was about to marry, was just getting ready to marry Lila's evil sister, Victoria. Amnesia interested me. I had never known anyone who had it, but the people on *All My Secrets* didn't seem surprised that this woman had suffered with the disease. I reached for my principal pad and wrote down the question, "Do people really get amnesia?" I might as well get as many questions as possible answered while I had the Emergency Line. I dialed the number.

"Psychic Emergency Line," a woman's voice said. "What kind of emergency are you experiencing?" She had an accent, like maybe she was from a South Sea island or something. I liked the way she sounded. "Do you want some choices to decide from?" I told her I did, and she went on. "We have matters of the heart, relationships with family and friends, employment, and financial matters."

"It's hard to say. I do have some questions about this guy I'm in love with, but there's more stuff that I need to know too." I glanced over at the TV screen. Lila and Jeff were wrapped in a tight hug.

* * * * *

"Ah," said the voice, "if you have multiple emergencies you need Madam Zelda. She is an expert on everything."

"Yes," I said. "Madam Zelda sounds great."

"Hello," said a lady with a soft voice. "This is Madam Zelda. With whom am I speaking?"

I sort of thought she ought to know, being psychic and all, but I told her, "Bird."

"Well, Bird, how can I help you?"

I thought I'd start with the easy question first, then go on. "Do people really get amnesia?" I asked.

"Ah, Madam Zelda hears a TV in the background. Are you watching *All My Secrets*?" I told her I was and she went on. "Very good! What is happening? We aren't allowed to watch on the job. I record it every day, but I don't want to wait until after work to find out how Jeff reacts when Lila comes home."

It seemed to me that Madam Zelda ought to know how Jeff would react, and it seemed like she shouldn't be spending my money finding out. I thought about saying so, but then I remembered that it was the school's money, so I might as well tell her. "They're doing a lot of kissing right now."

"Good," she said. "I hate the wicked Victoria."

"She does seem pretty awful, but do people really get amnesia very often?"

"Yes, yes indeed, but it is not a fate that will plague you, Bird."

"That's good. I have another question."

"Wait just a moment, Bird. I have just been informed by my supervisor that our office caller ID tells us you are calling on a school phone. This is not good. No one knows you are using our services, do they? We do not want trouble with a school making complaints to the Better Business Bureau."

"No," I lowered my voice because it carries so well. It occurred to me that someone in the outer office might hear me. "No one knows, but it is okay. I am the principal of this school."

"Really?" Madam Zelda sounded amazed. "We do not get many calls from principals, but my intuition tells me you are telling the truth. In fact I can see you in the principal's chair. You are new to the job, aren't you?"

"Yes, this is my first day.

"Ah, Madam Zelda sees that you may not last long in your position."

"That's for sure, just until Wednesday," I said, "but I want to ask you about this boy I'm in love with."

"You are in love with a boy? Is he a student? Psychic Emergency does not condone relationships of that sort between adults and children! We cannot advise about child abuse."

"No, no," I said. "It's not like that. We are the same age. I shouldn't have said boy, but, see, I am sort of young. This is my first job."

● ● ● ● ●

"Very well then. Tell me the young man's name, so that I can write it in my mind to bring forth the information about him."

"His name is Kash Edge, and he is so incredibly handsome that he should be a movie star."

"Ah, yes, Kash Edge. I see him clearly."

"You do! Isn't he a hottie?"

"Ah, yes, quite a nice looking young man. Madam Zelda would have been drawn to him herself in her younger days. What do you wish to know about this Kash?"

"Everything, no, I guess I just want to know if he will fall for me. See, he doesn't know yet that I love him."

"Ah, yes. I see that Kash will return your affections, but it is up to you to make the first move. I see that he does not yet think of you as a possible girlfriend."

"Oh," I squealed. "That's right! That's so right." I wanted to believe Madam Zelda. I liked what she said too much to doubt her. "So you think I should tell him? Just walk up to him, and say I'd like for us to be together?"

"Ah, not exactly," said Madam Zelda, "it is usually better in these matters to reveal your interest in a less direct way, one that will allow him to digest the information slowly."

"Like a note? Is that what you're saying, that I should write Kash a note?"

"Yes, a letter. That would be good or an e-mail."

"Thank you, Madam Zelda. You have been extremely

• • • • •

helpful." I was about to say good-bye when I remembered Katie's question. "Oh, there is one thing more."

"I am at your service," she said.

"Well, I have these friends. I used to be in a group with them. There were six of us, and we called ourselves the Six-Pack, but I had to move. Now they need a new member, and they were wondering if Emily or Beth would make the best replacement for me."

"Ah, and this group, they were all your true friends?"

I thought about lying, but if Madam Zelda was for real, she would know I was lying. If she was a fake, then I couldn't believe what she had said about Kash. "Not really, I guess. Katie is probably my only real friend in the group."

"Then why do you seek answers for them? Madam Zelda sees that this group is not a force for good. Tell your friend Katie to remove herself from the Six-Pack rather than seeking a replacement for you. You and the others, though young, are obviously too old to be acting like a bunch of ridiculous middle school girls!"

"I'll tell Katie. Thank you, Madam Zelda. Thank you very much." I hung up the phone and leaned back in my principal's chair. On TV, Victoria was bursting into the room to find Lila and Jeff kissing each other, but I couldn't get my mind on the program. I had too much to think about. Should I write Kash a note now? Of course, he wouldn't want to be involved with the principal. He might even tell someone who would get me in big trouble.

I could tell him the truth, but how do I know he wouldn't tell someone what was going on? I did want my two days in the office. The whole thing was really cool, and I did want to do something for Serenity. I was so deep in thought that when the phone rang, I jumped.

The white light was flashing. I pulled myself up straight in my chair to get back into character, and reached for the phone. "Yes, Mrs. Simpson, what is it?"

"It's about your lunch. I figured you might not want to tackle the lunchroom food on your first day, so I ordered out for us both. There's a place here in town that makes burritos on Mondays as their special, wonderful burritos, all covered with tomatoes. They are really good. It's my treat, sort of a welcoming present. Of course, if you don't like burritos, I am sure I can find a student who will eat yours. They should be here any minute. Does that sound good to you?"

A burrito did sound good. Usually I ate breakfast, and my stomach was starting to rumble with hunger. "Sounds great! Thank you, Mrs. Simpson."

"Good, and I want you to call me Nancy. I know I'm older than you are, but I'd feel more comfortable if you would use my first name."

Maybe I'd been wrong to think she didn't approve of me. "Thank you, Nancy."

"All right then. I'll give you a buzz when our food comes."

I went back to thinking about Kash. I started one note to him with, "I am not really the principal, but please do not tell anyone. I am actually in the eighth grade, just like you. I think you are incredibly handsome. If you decide we should go together, you can help me run the school until Wednesday." I stopped. I didn't want to promise Kash stuff like helping me run the school. If I did that, I wouldn't know if he really liked me or if he was just saying he did to get in on the fun. Besides, how could I let him help me run the school? I couldn't tell Mrs. Simpson that I was keeping the boy out of class all day just because I liked to look at him.

I was thinking maybe I would call Madam Zelda back, level with her about what I was doing, and ask if I should tell Kash. Then I started to wonder if the Psychic Emergency Line had to report crimes they heard about. Maybe they had some kind of deal like that with the police. I sure didn't want to be found out before Wednesday. After that, I would take my punishment, but I wanted every possible minute as the head of Thomas Jefferson Middle School.

Just then the phone rang, and the white light flashed. "Hannah Felder is here wanting to talk to you. She's the president of our Student Council. I told her you were busy, but she wants to know when she can come back to talk about some project for the council."

"Hum," I stalled. It might be good to talk to another kid. Maybe I could get some helpful information about

Serenity or even Kash. "No, it is absolutely all right to send her in. Nothing is more important to me than communicating with the students." Before I had replaced the phone, the door opened, and a pretty girl sort of bounced into my office. "Come in, Hannah," I said, but she was already sitting down across from me.

"Hello," she said. "I'm awful glad you are here. I'm the Student Council president, and we've been wanting to have an all-school project, sort of pull us all together. The thing is, though, everyone said we had to wait until we got a principal."

Hannah had big brown eyes and a smile like you might see on a toothpaste commercial. She seemed so full of energy that I sort of expected her to jump up and down in the chair.

I had known girls like Hannah back in Denver. "I'll bet you're not just the Student Council president. I'll bet you are a cheerleader." The surprised look on Hannah's face told me I was right, but I added, "Am I correct?"

"You are. That's awesome! You are real smart. I don't think Mr. Lawrence would have been able to guess that, if he didn't know me, I mean."

"Well," I said. "It wasn't so long ago that I was a middle school girl myself."

Hannah flashed me a smile. "I'm thinking it would be so cool if Thomas Jefferson got in the book of *World-Wide Records*."

"He's probably already in there for being the most famous person to mistreat slaves."

"Huh?" she said, then she caught on. "Oh, you mean the man, but I was talking about our school, us." She waved her arms to indicate she meant the whole school.

"What do you have in mind?"

"We wanted to do a water balloon fight, but some college had one with 5,214 balloons." She sighed deeply. "I don't believe we can beat that, do you?" I opened my mouth to agree, but she didn't wait. "So I want to try palindromes!"

I had heard the word, but I couldn't remember what it meant. "Tell me about it," I said, but Hannah was no bubble brain.

"You know what a palindrome is, don't you?"

I was about to lie and say I did when Hannah went on. "Oh, that's all right. My mother forgets things a lot too. She says it's her age."

I gave Hannah a dirty look. I mean, I wanted to seem old enough to be out of school and everything, but I didn't want to be identified with somebody's mother. "I am sure your mother is a good deal older than I am, Hannah," I said.

She shrugged. "Whatever, but let me tell you about the palindrome project." She talked fast now, so fast that I had to really focus on her words to stay up. "Oh, yeah, I didn't tell you. A palindrome is a word or phrase you can

· · · · · ·

spell backward and have it stay the same word, you know like my name, Hannah, or noon. Well anyway, I thought we could have the whole school make lists of palindromes, like at the same time. Then we could take all the lists and see how many different words we came up with. The thing is, I looked up the rules." She waved a piece of paper that I supposed contained the rules. "We've got to make an application to the book before we do our project. They have to decide if they are interested in the most palindromes listed by a school." She stopped talking suddenly and stared at me, waiting, I realized, for a comment from me.

"Umm," I said.

She started again, like a freight train getting up speed. "Well, it's a good idea, don't you think? I was pretty sure you would love the idea because it's educational and all, dealing with words. I mean a water balloon fight would have been more fun for us, students, teachers, even the cafeteria workers, but they had more than four hundred people and all those balloons. Besides my friend Julie, who is also on the Student Council, said no middle school principal would ever go for that." She stopped again and looked at me. When I didn't say anything, she started again fast. "So if it's okay, I'll fill out the application for palindromes." She pulled a piece of paper from her purse. "I've started my list. You don't think that is cheating, do you? Want to hear what I have so far?" She did not give me a chance to answer. "Peep, Bob, deed, level, did, mom, dad, sis, Anna, Nan, tot, noon. I mentioned that one already, and nun."

She slowed down enough for me to speak quickly. "That's wonderful, Hannah, but I am thinking about the water balloon fight. It might be something the council would like to do just for fun, as a sort of unifying activity."

She jumped from her chair, arms above her head, and I thought she was about to break into a cheer. "No Way!" she shouted. "That's so cool. When? When can we have the fight?"

All through Hannah's palindrome list, I had been planning the water balloon thing. It would be an awesome way to end my last day as principal. "Tomorrow," I said, "last period. I'll make the announcement after lunch. No one will be forced to join, of course, but everyone will be encouraged to participate for school spirit."

"You're wonderful!" Hannah was beginning to bounce toward the door. "We'll have it out behind the school, don't you think, you know where the grass is? We can use Student Council funds to buy the balloons. I'll get Mom to drive us to Ponca City to Big-Mart. Oh, Ms. Miller, I don't want to sound glad that Mr. Lawrence got sick or anything, but I'm like real glad you are here!"

With a deep sigh, I fell back into my chair. I had totally forgotten to ask Hannah about Serenity. Oh, well, I wasn't sure I could have directed Hannah to any topic she didn't

• • • • •

have on her mind. Hannah was not easy to lead. I had just a minute to rest before Mrs. Simpson called to say our burritos had arrived. "I'll be right out," I said. I hurried to the door, flung it open, and stared right into the face of Angie, the waitress from City Café.

Chapter 7

Nancy Simpson was busy digging into her purse for money, and Angie was waiting patiently. I wanted to go back into my office and slam the door, but I knew Angie had already seen me. I had to hope she wouldn't recognize me dressed like a principal, but she was staring at me while she chewed her gum.

"Smells wonderful," I said.

Angie didn't take her eyes off my face, just kept popping her gum and looking at me even when Nancy said, "Oh here it is. I knew I had a ten in here somewhere." She leaned across to hold the money out. "Keep the change, dear," she said, and then she looked up at Angie. I guess she noticed how Angie was staring at me. "Oh," she said, "You must be wondering who this is. We have Ms. Miller filling in for us until Mr. Lawrence can come back." Nancy turned her chair to look at me. "Ms. Miller, this is one of our former students, Angie Bradford. She just graduated from high school last spring, and now here she is bringing our lunch to us."

"I am glad to meet you, Angie," I said, and I held my breath.

She stepped away from Nancy's desk to be closer to me. She twisted her face and studied me. "You look familiar to me," she said.

I inched back toward the open office door even though I didn't yet have my burrito, and my stomach was growling. "I guess I have the same face a lot of people have, not very unusual," I said.

Angie shook her head. "Naw, it's more than that. I know I've seen you. You ever been in Judy's place?"

"Maybe," I said. "I'm not sure what cafés I've been in here."

"You been in a café in Prairie Dog Town, you been in Judy's. We're the only eating place in town 'cept the drive in."

"Umm," I said. It was a comment I have noticed that adults use a lot when they don't want to talk about something. All that inching had gotten me back to the open doorway. "I have lots of work to do," I stepped inside and started to close the door.

"Wait," said Nancy Simpson. "Your burrito. Here, Angie, will you take this to Ms. Miller?"

I moved quickly to get behind my desk. Maybe I would look more principal-like there, or maybe I should get down and hide in the space where my knees were supposed to go. I kept my head down, pretending to study Serenity's file that was still on my desk. "Thank you," I muttered when Angie placed the burrito on my desk. She did not leave my office, just stood there staring at me and chomping that gum.

"It really bugs me when I can't think why I know someone." She crossed her arms, and I had the feeling she planned to stay there in my office until she came up with the answer.

"Thank you again, Angie," I said, "but I'm afraid I need to get back to work. Will you please close the door on your way out?"

"No," she said, "I can't."

The girl was refusing to leave the principal's office! What nerve! I decided to yell at her, but before I could do it, she started talking again.

"I can't leave till I get your cup of ice tea. It's still on Mrs. Simpson's desk."

I sighed with relief. "Oh, yes, my drink." I got up and went to the door just as Angie walked out of my office. I closed the door behind her, but I stuck out my arm.

"You don't need to bother with coming back in. Just hand me the tea." I waved my arm until I felt the cup in my hand. Then I yelled. "And stop chewing that gum, Angie." I closed the door and leaned against it.

"She's kind of funny acting, ain't she?" I heard Angie say through the door.

Nancy didn't talk as loud as Angie. I cracked the door a

little to hear her say, "She's just young. Being a principal at her age must be scary. She's never even taught, just got her master's degree in administration."

"Oh," said Angie. "She going to be here all the time now?"

"No, Mr. Lawrence will be coming back. I imagine Ms. Miller will need to teach for a while before she can get a full-time job as principal."

"She'd be kind of pretty if she knew how to dress," Angie said. "'Course, she'd have to do something with that hair too. She sure does look familiar, though."

I made a face at Miss Fashion Critic, but I did it behind the door. Next I turned on the TV. I wanted to find something to watch while I ate. My choices were soap operas and news. I settled on *Specific Hospital,* the soap that came on after *All My Secrets.* I didn't know anything at all about the plot, but it didn't take long to catch on. A character named Mariah was being arrested for murder. It didn't look good for her because she had previously been blackmailed by Brad, the dead man. I got kind of interested while I ate. My burrito tasted really great. I licked my fingers when I finished. That's when a knock sounded on my door, and before I could say anything a man came bursting into my office.

He wore gym shorts and had a whistle around his neck. He nodded to me. "Hi, I'm Coach Pickle, Bill Pickle, actually. Can you imagine anyone with the name of Pickle calling their child Bill? I guess it was meant to make me tough, kind of like that 'Boy Named Sue' song." He must have seen from my face that I didn't know what he was talking about. "Remember, the old Johnny Cash song where a boy's dad names him Sue so he will learn to fight?"

I nodded even though I had no idea what he was talking about, and he plopped down in the chair. His eyes went toward the TV. "*Specific Hospital!* Great! I love this show. Why is Mariah being arrested?"

I explained about the murder charge. The coach shook his head. "She didn't do it," he said. "I know Mariah too well to believe that!"

I told him that I could see she seemed too nice, and for a while we just watched. I felt a little funny at first, but then I could see that Coach Pickle was really enjoying himself even during the commercials. He explained to me that this was his preparation period. "I'm not leaving a class unsupervised," he said.

One of the sponsors of the show was the Psychic Emergency Line, and I told him that I had used their services. When the program was over, he turned his chair back to face me. "Hannah Felder is telling all around school that you are letting Student Council plan a water balloon fight for tomorrow."

"That's right. I am going to make an announcement about it in a few minutes." I drew myself up, ready for a fight. "Do you think it's a bad idea?"

I was relieved when he shook his head. "No objection here," he said. "Of course some of the others may complain. You know we have some real stuffed shirts teaching here. Some of these teachers assign a lot of homework too. Me? I think we need to leave the homework to the schools in foreign countries."

I smiled at him. "Glad to hear we think alike," I said, and I hoped again that I'd get in Coach Pickle's class when I became a student.

He stood up. "Just wanted to know if the balloon fight was really going to come down. I might give my boys some tips on water balloons in the gym this afternoon." He sort of leaned across the desk, closer to me. "Rumor is that you're single," he said. "That true too?"

We were getting on shaky ground. I nodded.

"Me too," he said. "There aren't many of us singles in Prairie Dog Town. Maybe we could take in a movie or something over at Ponca one of these days."

I stared at him. The man was at least forty! "No," I shook my head. "not me. My mother, though, she might go out with you."

"Your mother!" He moved toward the door. "I'm not taking out the mother of anyone I work for." He went out the door shaking his head. I wondered if that meant he wouldn't be coming back tomorrow to watch *Specific Hospital* with me.

I wanted to spend more time with Serenity, but I didn't

know what I could say to help her. I thought of asking Mrs. Simpson for advice, but that would not be good for the image I was working for. There was only one thing to do. I reached for the phone and dialed the Psychic Emergency Line. This time I asked for Madam Zelda right off.

"Hello, Bird," she said. "Still in the principal's office are you?"

"I am, but I have a problem you can help me with."

"Shoot," said Madam Zelda.

"Well, there's this girl, see. Her name is Serenity, but don't get the idea she is calm or anything." I thought Madam Zelda should be impressed that I knew the meaning of serene, but then I remembered that I was supposed to be this big-time principal. Principals usually know what the word means, although I can't say that I've ever seen one who was, serene, I mean. "Serenity makes things up, exaggerates all the time. I guess she does it for attention. Like, she said in history class this morning that Marilyn Monroe was her real mother."

"Impossible," said Madam Zelda.

"Right, which is exactly what one of the girls said. I guess she probably said a lot more than that it wasn't possible. She made some crack about how stupid Serenity is. There is a group of girls who pick on her all the time. Well, anyway Serenity pops the girl one, right there in math class, so of course, she ended up in the principal's office."

"With you?"

"Yeah, and I don't know what to say to Serenity. I really want to help her."

Madam Zelda made a sort of sad clucking sound with her tongue. "Tsk-tsk, have you ever thought, Bird, how middle school is like the *Titanic*? Otherwise nice people behave like savages, afraid someone will get on their life boat."

I was amazed. The woman could really read my mind. "I said just that same thing to Serenity this morning!"

"You did? I mean, of course, you did, but back to your question, how to help this poor child, Serenity." She started to make a sort of chanting sound, "Ommmm, let me get in touch with my inner knowledge."

I waited for what seemed like a long time. The line was quiet. "Madam," I said, "you are still there, aren't you?"

"I am, Bird. Madam will not desert you, not as long as your phone line stays open, but I am afraid this call is going to be expensive. Madam has to think."

"Oh, don't worry about the charges. The school will pay for them. What better thing for a principal to spend money on than expert advice on how to help a troubled kid."

"Well, yes, of course." She started the chanting sound again. Finally she spoke. "The girl needs confidence, Bird, confidence and a friend."

"Uh-huh," I said, "go on."

"Do you have anything on you, anything like a necklace or charm?"

My hand went to the chain I wore around my neck. It

* * * * *

was inside my jacket, but at the end of that chain was my Six-Pack charm, the little can. "I do," I said. "I have a chain with a little charm on it."

"Very good. Give the necklace to Serenity. Tell her that each time she is teased she should touch the necklace. Tell her the charm is magic and will make her able to hold up her head and make it unnecessary for her to seek attention by exaggerating."

The old "this sword is magic and can slay dragons" tale. It sounded good in a story, but I didn't think Serenity would fall for it. I mean the girl wasn't stupid, well, not in most ways, anyway. "Is that all you've got, Madam?" I asked.

She made the sad tsk sound again. "It is, Bird, for right now at least, I am afraid it is. You could call Madam back tomorrow. Maybe I could do some looking tonight on the Internet."

"The Internet?" I was beginning to doubt Madam again.

"Yes," she said, "even we psychics have to use the information highway on occasion. You try the magic necklace thing and get back to me if it doesn't work."

"I don't know. I don't think Serenity will believe that story. Besides, that necklace is what the girls gave me when I became a member of the Six-Pack, you know the group I told you about."

"Ah, yes," said Madam, "that wonderful group where you had only one true friend."

I did not want to discuss the Six-Pack with Madam. In

· · · · ·

125

that way she was too much like my mother. "Well," I said, "I've got work to do, principal stuff and all."

"Before you hang up, let me ask about the young man, Kash, I believe you said his name is. Have you made any progress with Kash?"

"Not yet."

"Perhaps you should ask Kash to help you with Serenity. Ah yes! That's it. Ask Kash to help you and let him know you like him."

"Well, I don't know."

"You do as Madam Zelda says." She sounded sort of put out with me.

"Okay, I will. Oh, yeah, I need to know something about global warming."

"Madam Zelda is not in favor of global warming."

"What is it? Give me a short explanation, sort of in a nutshell."

"Madam Zelda cannot be expected to know everything. Look it up on the Internet."

"Right, the information highway."

As soon as I put down the phone, I did use the computer in my office to get on the Internet and learn about global warming. I didn't understand much, but I scribbled down some quick notes. I might not be able to impress Kash with my knowledge, but at least if I was ever in a beauty pageant, which wasn't likely, but if I was, I would have a cause to discuss. "I'm deeply concerned about global warming,"

I imagined myself saying, and I was certain the audience would applaud me.

The white light came on, and the phone rang. I wanted to tell Mrs. Simpson that I was busy learning about global warming, but I didn't. "Ms. Miller," she said. "I've had several teacher's get on the intercom to ask me if it is true that we are having a schoolwide water balloon fight tomorrow. It isn't, is it?"

I remembered Miss Deirdre. Think the thought, I told myself, and I started thinking what Principal Bird would be thinking. The kids are going to love this balloon stuff. The teachers aren't. Well, that's tough, the teachers have had their way plenty.

"Mrs. Simpson," I said, "I was just about to make an announcement about that very thing." I thought I sounded very principalish.

"You do remember how to use the PA system, don't you?" She sounded like I was an eighth-grader or something.

"I do, thank you Mrs. Simpson." I used her last name on purpose.

"So you are going to put a stop to this nonsense about water balloons, aren't you?"

"Thank you for your concern, Mrs. Simpson, but I am the principal. I will handle this." I said, and I hung up the phone, totally sure that outside my door was one very angry lady.

• • • • •

I made some notes on my principal's pad, then scooted my chair over to the public address system, drew in my breath, and reached for the all-call button. You're young, I told myself, but you've studied all that principal stuff, and you for sure know what you are doing. It will build school spirit for the student body and faculty to have fun together. Now make your announcement.

"All right, Prairie Dogs," I said, "I want to talk to you about the event sponsored by your student council tomorrow afternoon. No one will have to go to last period class. That's cool, huh?" I paused for a minute and could imagine kids clapping all over the building. "Okay, at two thirty, all those who want to participate will go out to the back of the building. Our able student council members will have water balloons filled. Take two at a time, and throw them at the person of your choice." I noticed from the corner of my eye that Mrs. Simpson had come into the office, and she was staring at me, her mouth open. I gave her what I hoped was a "Don't question me look," and went on with my announcement. "There are no winners or losers at this game, just lots of fun. I like to think that all the Prairie Dogs in this school are winners." I was so proud of that line that I repeated it. "Yes, indeed, all our Prairie Dogs are winners. Now, it goes without saying," I liked that phrase too. "It goes without saying that no student, member of the faculty, or staff will be forced to participate. If you don't want to have fun with the rest of us, just report to the library and do research. I suggest you read up on global warming, a problem that has recently been brought to my attention and which deeply concerns me. Now back to the balloons. Don't worry about getting wet. A little water never hurt anyone, and our weather is really warm for the last day of October. Just bring towels and extra clothes if you want to change. Oh, I almost forgot tonight is Halloween. I hope you all have fun and don't eat any poisoned candy or anything. Over and out."

"This is crazy," Mrs. Simpson said from behind me when I had switched off the all-call button.

I turned my chair around slowly to look her in the face. All the time I turned, I tried to think thoughts a principal would think, but I was mad. "Go back to your desk," I said, "you aren't the boss of me."

Thank heavens Miss Deirdre didn't hear that last comment. I knew it sounded more like a three-year-old than a principal, but I remembered no actor is perfect. Anyway, Mrs. Simpson stormed back to her desk, shaking her head and muttering to herself as she slammed the door.

Next I remembered that Madam Zelda had suggested I write Kash a note. I took my principal's pad and started to write. "Dear Kash, You may think it is strange to get a note from me, but I just want to tell you that I think you are just the hottest boy I have ever met. Now, I know you are thinking that I am way too old for you, but you would be surprised to know how close I am to your age. Don't show anyone this note or talk about it or anything. Just think about it for a couple of days. Maybe we will get a chance to discuss our relationship on Wednesday. I think on that day you may see me as a whole different person from the person you see me as today, if you know what I mean, and you probably don't. You will, though, I promise. Anyway, just give the idea some thought. If you knew a girl who was a whole lot like me, except that she was in the eighth grade with you, could you maybe want her for your girlfriend? Yours sincerely, Robin 'Bird' Miller. P.S. Thank you for cluing me in to the hazards of global warming. We can discuss the problem anytime you want to."

I read back over the note. I wasn't sure I should give it to him, but Madam Zelda had been absolutely sure I should. Of course, Madam Zelda had also said I should give Serenity my Six-Pack charm. If I believed she was right about Kash, I had to believe she was right about Serenity. I would take the note to the grocery store after school, buy some candy to give out on Halloween, and hand Kash the note when he bagged my purchases.

Now I needed to think about Serenity. I picked up the phone. "Have Serenity Blair sent down here."

"Yes, ma'am," said Mrs. Simpson, and her voice was icy. "Oh, and I might mention that several teachers have asked that you meet with the entire faculty and staff immediately after school."

A room full of teachers looking at me! No amount of

remembering Miss Deirdre's instruction could get me through that. I didn't want to be discovered. I wanted my other day as principal. "You may inform my staff that I am truly sorry, but I have other obligations this afternoon. We could have a meeting after school tomorrow except that everyone will be wet, and that wouldn't be comfortable, would it? The faculty meeting will have to be postponed until Wednesday, and I have a feeling they won't want to meet with me then." I laughed. "I mean, you know everyone will be too tired by Wednesday to stick around here for a meeting."

"Whatever you say. You're in charge, at least for now."

"Thank you, Nancy, and don't forget to send for Serenity," I said.

"You need not worry about my forgetting. I, for one, take my job very seriously, and call me Mrs. Simpson, please." She hung up the phone.

In just a few minutes, Serenity opened my office door. She had a tissue in her hand, and her nose was red from crying. "Sit down," I said, "and tell me what's wrong."

She shrugged her shoulders, a habit that was really beginning to get on my nerves. Oh, sure, I'd heard teachers jump on kids for shrugging instead of speaking when they were called on. I was dimly aware that my own mother had complained about me doing the same thing, but still I wanted to slap Serenity. I didn't, but my voice got stern without even going over Miss Deirdre's "think

• • • • •

the thought" rule. "Listen to me, girl. I am trying to help you here, but you have got to drop that shrugging stuff. Got me?" She nodded. "Head movements are better than shoulder movements, but what I really want is speech, Serenity. Open your mouth and talk to me."

"Yes, Ms. Miller," she said.

"Good, now, let's try again. Why have you been crying, Serenity?"

"It's the balloon fight. Everyone's all excited about it. They can't wait for it, but I'll have to go to the library and do research about global warming."

"Why?"

"If I go outside and try to have fun with the others, Nicole and her group will all gang up on me. They'll hit me with all of their balloons."

"*Hummmmm,*" I said. I could understand her point. I tried not to see it, but pictures of me with the Six-Pack flashed into my mind. I could see us all hurling big water balloons at Marcy Willis. I reached for my pad and wrote, "Call Hannah Felder down here and tell her she has to get small balloons."

"See what I mean," said Serenity. "You know it's the truth, don't you?"

"Serenity, what you need is someone to stand beside you, someone to remind you that you don't need to exaggerate, someone to fight back with you. You need a friend."

She rolled her eyes. "Duh, like I didn't know that. Most of this started after Ashley dropped me and became one of the Purples."

"Well, you have a friend now." I reached up and unfastened the chain from around my neck. "Take this necklace and wear it. Every time you feel tempted to exaggerate, touch the necklace and say to yourself, 'I have a friend. I do not need to impress these people. They would not believe me anyway.'"

"Yeah, but who's my friend? If I tell myself I have one, I'm just making stuff up like before."

The girl was thick headed. "Pay attention here. I'm your friend!"

"You're the principal. You have to be everyone's friend. What good will it do me to have a friend in the principal's office."

"It will do you good. You just wait to see what happens tomorrow at the water balloon fight. Yes, indeed [I was proud of coming up with that phrase], you go right on and plan to join the fun. I promise you will enjoy it." Serenity smiled for a minute, and I noticed she looked kind of pretty when she did. A brilliant idea came to me. "A new girl is coming to our school on Wednesday. She and her mother came in to enroll earlier today." I shook my head and made my face look sad. "Shy little thing. She goes by the nickname, Bird, and I have to say it fits her. She looks like she might fly away if someone gets too

• • • • •

close. She will need you, Serenity. In fact I took the liberty [boy, I was getting good at principal talk] of telling her about you."

"You told her I make things up and that everyone picks on me?"

I sighed. "Touch your necklace, dear. You are exaggerating again, aren't you? We've already established that not everyone picks on you, and no I did not mention those things to Bird. I simply said that you were a very bright and kind girl, and that I would ask you to show her around the school, help her find her classes and everything."

"Well, sure, I can do that, but she won't want to come near me after she sees how Nicole and the Purples treat me."

"I think you are wrong. I feel this girl, Bird, has been through some experiences that have made her wiser than the average girl. You just wait and see."

Serenity didn't say anything. I knew she was telling herself not to get her hopes up, but the corners of her mouth kept trying to turn up into a smile. "Are you doing anything to celebrate Halloween tonight?"

"Nah, just staying home and giving out candy. I've got to watch our yard and house real close. It would be just like the Purples to throw eggs all over the porch or toilet paper the trees."

"We'll make them pay tomorrow." I put back my arm like I was throwing, *"Splash! Splash! Splash!"* I said, then I thought maybe that didn't sound very much like a principal. "Well," I said, "what goes around, comes around, if you know what I mean."

Serenity left my office at three. The schedule I found in my desk said school was dismissed at three fifteen. I didn't have much time, but I wanted to call Katie because it was two in Denver, exactly between classes.

"Hello," she was talking loud already. "Why haven't you called me back?"

"Katie," I said, "I've got a school to run here. I've been busy."

"Oh," she screamed, "you're still the principal! For real?"

"For real, but don't talk so loud. If a teacher should hear you, they'd make you tell where I am, and they'd call and everything."

"Promise me you are telling the truth. Ivory thinks you're making up stories to get attention."

"You've got me mixed up with Serenity," I said, but I knew Katie didn't know what I meant. "Never mind. Yes, I promise I'm telling the truth, but Katie, you want to hear something? I don't care what Ivory thinks! I wish you wouldn't either."

There was a long silence. Then Katie said, "Well, tell me what's been happening."

I told her about the soap opera and the coach. I told her about calling the Psychic Emergency Line, and I told her about writing the note for Kash. I did not tell her about Serenity. I knew I would tell her, but not today.

"Did you ask the psychic who we should invite to be in the Six-Pack with us?"

"I did, but she told me she couldn't get a reading on that one. See Madam Zelda explained to me that she doesn't know everything. Actually she uses the Internet for lots of information, but, Katie, she did say you should break away from the Six-Pack."

"That's pretty easy for you to say. You're way off in Oklahoma. You know what the group would do to me if I quit them."

I couldn't argue with that. "Well," I said, "I am just repeating what Madam Zelda told me." Before we hung up, I had something to ask her. "Katie," I said, "will you find out a phone number for me?"

"Sure. Whose do you want?"

"Marcy Willis's. I need Marcy's phone number really bad."

"Marcy Willis!" Katie's voice was loud again. "Why on earth would you want her phone number?"

"I don't have time to explain right now, but please get it for me. Will you?"

"Well, I can try."

"Good! I'll call you tomorrow."

"Wait! Ivory told me to ask if you will send back the Six-Pack necklace?"

I pretended not to hear. It was five after three. I had to move fast. I grabbed up the note to Kash still on my principal's pad, turned off the light, and stepped out of my office. Mrs. Simpson was on the phone, but she said "just a minute," to the person on the other end.

"I'm leaving early today," I told her.

She lifted her eyebrows. "Leaving early? Well, you might want to come early too. Tuesday is cinnamon roll day in the cafeteria. They are wonderful, and they will be ready just in time for the teachers' meeting."

"Teachers' meeting?"

"Yes, in the library before school."

"Of course," I said like the meeting was my idea, but I knew my voice sounded scared. I started toward the door, but remembered something important. "By the way, Mrs. Simpson, please send Hannah Felder a note saying I want her to buy small balloons for tomorrow's . . ." I searched for a word. "Festival. Yes, that's it. We need small balloons for the festival." I turned again to leave.

"Your key," called Mrs. Simpson. I looked back to see her holding out a key on a ribbon. "This is a master key," she said like she was talking to an incredibly slow person. "That means it opens every door in the building. You will need to be careful with it."

"Well, duh," I said. Then I made for the door, fast.

Rendi was in the sunroom, putting away the few things she'd brought with her from her studio. She had the radio playing kind of loud, and she hadn't heard me come into the house. I stood for a minute in the sunroom doorway, watching her. I had real mixed feelings, and I leaned against the doorframe. I had already told her I was sorry about what we did to Marcy, and part of me wanted to let her know that I had forgiven her for dragging me away from Denver. Part of me even wanted to tell her what a great day I had, but, of course, I couldn't do that. Besides, I wasn't ready to let her off the hook yet. She hated for me to be mad at her. Maybe I could use that somehow when she found out what I was up to at school. She was bound to find out, and I was pretty sure her reaction wouldn't be pretty. No, it was definitely better to remain distant with her until the news broke.

I stepped into the room, and she turned to look at me, putting down some tools. "Bird! You're home. How did it go? Tell me about it? Do I need to go up and sign anything?"

I made my face look expressionless. "No. There's no need for you to go up, and there's not much to tell." I shrugged (oh, sure I know I had decided to give that up, but it fit so well here). "Just like any other miserable first days in a strange school." I gave a bitter little laugh. "No, this one was truly worse. These kids actually seemed afraid of me, and the teachers didn't even like me, except one coach." I thought of saying that the coach had tried to hit on me, had actually asked me out. I didn't tell that, though. I knew Rendi would be calling the school on that one. When they put her through to the principal, she would recognize my voice.

· · · · ·

She frowned. "I'm sorry you feel that way, honey. Maybe tomorrow will be better."

"Tonight is Halloween," I said. "I'm missing Ivory's party."

"You can call the girls if you want to," she said. "Maybe that will make you feel better."

I sighed long and sad. "No. Thank you, though, for giving me a chance to talk to my real friends. I think it would just make me too lonely right now. We don't have anything in the house to give to trick-or-treaters. Do you want me to walk to the grocery store to get some candy?"

"No, let's go out to Judy's and eat, if you're hungry. I didn't have any lunch, and I'm starved. We can stop at the grocery on the way back for candy."

"Judy's restaurant? I don't want to eat there."

"Why? It's the only place in town."

"Yeah," I said, and I rolled my eyes. "I am aware of that, believe me. I mean I know how tiny this place is."

"The food was good, remember, and Judy is so nice. She'll be glad to see us there. Go put on your jeans. You'll feel better when you get out of that suit. Honey, those things you bought make you look at least ten years older. It's little wonder the kids at school may have been sort of standoffish with you. Wouldn't you like to take back the ones you haven't worn?"

"Maybe I will take three of them back," I said, "but I want to wear one more tomorrow."

● ● ● ● ●

"Why do you want to wear one more?"

I shrugged and admitted to myself that I could never give it up, not while I was still a kid. Rendi went back to the subject of eating. "Come on, go change, and let's go to Judy's. I remember seeing a sign when we were there the other day about the burrito special they have on Mondays."

"I don't want another burrito. I mean, that's what the cafeteria served today," I said, but then I thought, maybe Angie wouldn't be at Judy's. She couldn't work night and day could she? Besides with different clothes and my hair down, she probably wouldn't connect me with school. It might be sort of fun to play with her mind. "Okay," I said. "I'll go change."

"Good," said Rendi when I came out. "You look more like my Bird now."

I had taken the notepad with the note still on it from my jacket pocket and put it carefully into the back pocket of my jeans. It might get wrinkled there, but not like the terrible way it would have in a front pocket. It had occurred to me while I was getting dressed that I wasn't likely to get a chance to deliver it now anyway. I couldn't go into the grocery store dressed as a kid. Kash Edge was definitely brighter than Angie and probably a lot more observant. I took it along, though, in case an opportunity came up.

It did. We were near the grocery store when Rendi said, "You know we might as well stop for the candy first, since we're right here. Do you want to run in to get it?"

"No," I said. "I just saw some kids going in there. I don't want to see anyone else from Thomas Jefferson Middle School today. You do it, please."

Rendi pulled the car into a parking space and got out. Just then I saw Kash! He rode up to the front of the store on a bike. What a sight! His hair glowed like gold in the afternoon sun. He had changed out of his school clothes. He wore khaki shorts and a blue T-shirt. I wished I could have been close enough to see if the shirt made his eyes look totally blue, but then I would have been close enough for him to see me. As it was, I leaned back close against the car seat. Kash never looked in my direction.

He rested his bike against the building. My mind raced. There was a basket on the bike. I could put the note in the basket, but how could I be sure Kash would notice a piece of paper lying in the basket? The wind was blowing, sweeping down the plain, just like in the song. The note might even blow out and never be seen by those dreamy blue-green eyes.

Then I saw it! Right outside my window was a rock. It was exactly the right size, not huge, but big enough to be noticed. "You wonderful rock," I said to myself, and in no time I was out the door, had the rock in my hand, and was headed toward the bike.

Rotten luck! Just as I reached it, the door of the grocery store opened and out stepped Serenity Blair. She had a bag in her arms, and I could see a loaf of bread sticking

* * * * *

out the top. "Wow, Ms. Miller!" she said. "You sure look different in jeans."

I pulled myself up straight and reached in my mind for the Principal Miller. "Good afternoon, Serenity,"

The girl just stood there staring at me. "Why you got a rock in your hand?" I could feel the principal inside me getting aggravated.

"I collect them," I said. "Now, Serenity, if there is nothing more you need to say, maybe you should step out of the doorway. Someone else may want to come out, and no doubt you should get home with your groceries and everything." I waited for her to speak, but she said nothing. "Go, Serenity!" I yelled, and I pointed my arm off toward where our car was parked.

"Okay, okay," she said, "but if it's all right with you, I'll go in the other direction. That's toward my house."

"By all means [good phrase, huh?]. Go in the direction of your house."

She started to move, but she turned back when she had taken only a few steps. "I wish the kids at school could see you like that," she said.

They'll get a chance, I thought, but I didn't let Serenity in on the information. Instead I moved toward the door like I was going in. When she rounded the corner and was out of sight, I stepped back, took the note from my pocket, stashed it in the basket, and laid the rock on it.

In the car again, I leaned back against the seat, but I

• • • • •

couldn't get comfortable. I shifted myself around. That note was so confusing. What good would it do? But Madam Zelda had told me to let him know. I pulled the pad from my back pocket. "Kash," I wrote. "Someone really likes you. You will find out who your admirer is before long."

I grabbed the door handle, jumped from the van, and ran to the bike. I moved the rock, stuffed the first note in my pocket, put down the new one, and replaced the rock. I still had my hands on the bike when Rendi came out the door with a bag in her arms, but I didn't know she was there until she said, "Bird?"

I jumped away from the bike. "Oh, you're ready to go, huh? I was just looking at this bike. It's nice, don't you think?"

Rendi smiled at me. "I saw the boy who rode up on that just as I was going in. I'd bet you were more interested in him than in his bike. His dad owns this store, and he works in there. He told me he was in the eighth grade. Anyway, he said kids his age trick-or-treat here. Just walk around town having a good time. I thought—"

"Mother!" I screamed. "You didn't mention me to him. Tell me that you didn't or I'll die!"

She handed me the bag of candy. "Calm down. I didn't say a word about you, knew you wouldn't like it. I wanted to say, 'I have the cutest daughter out in the car. Why don't you go out there and ask her to go trick-or-treating with you tonight?'"

* * * * *

"Puh-leeze, Mother." I rolled my eyes, but all the time I was getting in the van I couldn't help picturing it, Kash and me, maybe in matching costumes, something like Bert and Ernie. I wouldn't want to be a stupid princess or anything. No, we would look cute as a team. I wasn't sure I'd ever seen Bert and Ernie masks. Maybe we would have to paint our faces. Kash could be Bert with a yellow face. We'd need a sort of reddish color for my face. I was still daydreaming about it when we stopped in front of the café.

I got scared. "There aren't any other cars," I said. "You know they always say don't go to restaurants if there are no cars parked outside."

"We know the food's good, honey." She turned the car in to park in front. "There aren't any other cars because it's just after four, too early for most people." We got out. Just before Rendi opened the door, I told myself to forget the principal. You're Bird now, a rotten teenager who hates this town. I felt myself slouch.

"Hey, here come my girls." Judy waved at us from behind the counter. I didn't see Angie anywhere, and I didn't know whether to feel relieved or disappointed. Judy came over to take our order.

Mom ordered a burrito, and I said, "Me too," when Judy looked at me.

"I guess your burritos smell pretty good," Mom said to Judy. "Bird told me she didn't want one because they served them today in the cafeteria."

● ● ● ● ●

"Really?" Judy raised her eyebrows. "I've never heard of Doris Davis trying to make burritos. I've known Doris forever, think the world and all of her, but," she lowered her voice like someone might hear us, "the woman can't cook." She laughed. "Not a good thing for the head of the entire school cafeteria. Mind you, she's got a heart as big as Texas, but cinnamon rolls are the only thing she can make." She reached out and patted my shoulder. "Don't you go repeating what I said about her cooking."

"Oh, I won't. I know how important secrets can be."

When Judy brought our food, she sat down in the booth beside Rendi. "I'm all ready for the dinner crowd," she said. "Bird, you tell me what you thought of our middle school."

I looked down at my burrito. I didn't know how to answer. I didn't want to hurt Judy's feelings by saying stuff about how I hated the school, but I didn't want to change the story I'd told Rendi either. "Well," I said, "one of the things I like best is the principal. She's just a substitute, I guess."

"That's right, David Lawrence has to be out for a while on account of his heart surgery."

"I can sure see why he might have heart trouble," I said. "Being the principal of a middle school is awful hard." I noticed how surprised Rendi looked. "Well, it is," I said. "You probably don't even know it, but I think about things like that."

* * * * *

Rendi grinned and sort of looked down. I wasn't sure what the smile meant. "Tell us about this interim principal," she said, but before I had a chance to talk, she looked at Judy and added, "You see, it is rather unusual for Bird to take to a school administrator or for them to truly enjoy her."

I shrugged. "I don't know. I talked to her when I enrolled. She's real young for one thing. I think that probably helps her understand kids. Today was her first day at the school, just like me."

"Heard they'd got some young woman from the city," said Judy. "Wonder where she's living. Sort of thought she might want to rent my place. 'Course that was before you two came. I'd rather have you."

I smiled at Judy around my bite of burrito. I was on a roll, though, and I wanted to say more about the principal. "Oh," I said, "I almost forgot. Her name is Robin Miller, just like mine. Isn't that wild, two Robin Millers coming to that little school on the same day?" I bent my head to one side and looked up at the ceiling, thinking. "You know, there was something real familiar about her. She couldn't be a relative or something, could she, Rendi?"

"No, I didn't name you after a relative, Bird."

I was kind of bummed out about how Rendi had told Judy about my trouble with principals. I thought of a way to get even. "Oh, yeah, I forgot you named me Robin because your mother said she didn't want her granddaughter named for a bird." A sudden understanding came to me. "Hey, that's why you called me 'Bird' right off, wasn't it, to get at Grandma?" Rendi's face turned red, and I was sort of sorry I had embarrassed her. "See, Judy, my grandparents always wanted to tell Rendi how to raise me. That's why we don't have much to do with them."

Judy smiled. "Never works for the older generation to go trying to tell grown-up kids what to do." She reached out and sort of patted Rendi's hand. "Kind of a shame, though, not having your folks part of your lives." She might have said more, but just then the front door swung open, and in came Angie.

"Hi, everyone," she called out. I had lost my nerve and no longer wanted to see her. I held my breath, hoping she would go on back to the kitchen, but she didn't.

She came over to lean against our booth on Rendi's side. "Oh, yeah," she said. "You're the two who had the run-in with our deputy. You get settled into your new home yet?"

I didn't even listen to Rendi's answer. Just kept my eyes down, and shoveled the burrito into my mouth, hoping that would keep anyone from asking me any questions.

"You start to school yet?" I heard the question, but I pretended not to, just kept eating.

"Yes," said Rendi, "Bird went to school today, but she

seems to be too busy scarfing down Judy's great burrito to answer."

I swallowed and said, "Oh, yeah, I went."

Angie leaned close to me. "You meet that weird principal?"

I nodded my head, but I didn't look up, just kept on chewing. "Just wondered," said Angie. She walked back toward the kitchen then, and I glanced up. She turned back twice to stare at me, her face screwed up in thought.

We were almost finished with our burritos when Sheriff Walters came in and headed for our booth. "Put your hands in the air," he said, but he laughed. "Just funning you." He took off his cap and used it to tap my shoulder. "Scoot over Sparrow, and I'll join y'all."

"The girl's name is Bird, Clyde," said Judy. I looked at Rendi, expecting her to say we were finished, but she was smiling. I scooted over, and the sheriff joined us. Angie had his burrito and ice tea there before he was completely settled.

"You been chiseling away?" the sheriff asked Rendi.

She told him then about how she didn't chisel out of stone and how she builds a framework and takes it to a foundry to get it cast. "I'll be able to work metal by hand too as soon as my tools arrive." Judy and the sheriff seemed majorly interested in sculpting. Rendi told them how she had pieces in shows and museums and how that is the way she sells things and even has people ask her to make special pieces for them. She ended up by saying she hadn't sold anything much lately. "I may be asking Judy for a job here by December," she said.

Talk turned to Halloween. "Oh, yeah, tonight's a busy night for me," said the sheriff. "I've even got a deputy coming in to help me patrol, make sure none of the kids get carried away."

After a while, Rendi did say we needed to go. Judy and Sheriff Walters stood up to let us out. We were on our way over to pay Angie when the Sheriff said. "Reckon you've talked to your mama and daddy by now, asked them to come and see you."

"Not yet," said Rendi, and she kept walking.

Angie took Rendi's money. "Hey," she said. "I got it! That new principal at the middle school! She looks just like you!" She turned to Rendi. "You got to go up there and see her! It will flat-out amaze you."

"I'll do that," said Rendi. "Maybe tomorrow."

"See," I said when we were out the door, "I told you there was something familiar about the principal. I guess she does look kind of like me. Isn't that amazing, the same name too!" Then I added like it was an afterthought. "You can't see her tomorrow. I heard someone say she would be in meetings all day with the superintendent."

All the way to our house, I worried over Kash coming to our house. At first I thought I would go straight to bed when we got home, tell Rendi I had a headache or something, but the more I thought about it the more I wanted to see Kash Edge. I wondered what kind of costume he would have on. I just had to see how those awesome blue-green eyes looked in the light of our porch lamp, but if I saw him it had to be as Ms. Miller.

At home, I went right in and changed back into the suit I had worn to school. When I came out of my room, I went into the kitchen where Rendi was putting some little candy bars from the packages she had bought into a big bowl. "Why'd you change back into that outfit?" she asked me.

I shrugged. "Just wanted to," I said.

Rendi shook her head. "You're a strange Bird," she said, and she reached out to hug me, "but I like you just the way you are."

I gave away an entire bowl of candy, mostly to little kids. There were a few who looked about my age, but they must not have seen me at school because they didn't pay any particular attention to me. I kept my eye on the clock. Maybe Kash wasn't coming after all, but at about eight he did.

Somehow I knew when he knocked, just knew that Kash Edge stood outside on our porch, and I couldn't go to the door. "Will you get this one?" I called to Rendi who was stretched out on the couch watching TV.

"Bird," she said, "this movie is getting good," but she got up and was almost to the door when I changed my mind. I couldn't let her go to the door and then call me over to talk about how I was new in school and all.

"Go back to your movie," I told her. I grabbed the candy bowl, rushed past her, took a deep breath, and opened the door.

He was standing there with another boy. The other kid didn't have on any kind of costume, but Kash had a long, fake beard and a black felt hat pulled down over his ears. He must have been trying for a hillbilly look because he had a corncob pipe in his hand. He wore overalls, fastened over just one shoulder with a torn sleeveless shirt under them. He looked so hot, like the hottest hillbilly in the world!

"It's the new principal," I heard Kash whisper under his breath. Then he took off his hat and sort of bowed to me. "Howdy, ma'am. I didn't expect to see you." He scratched at his head. "There was another lady invited me to come by here for trick or treats, said she lived here with her daughter."

"That was my sister." I kept my voice low in case Rendi could hear, but I looked over my shoulder and saw that she was all into her movie again.

"Think she kind of wanted us to meet her daughter," Kash said. "Is she to home?"

He was talking in an adorable hillbilly voice. "My niece isn't here right now, but I know you will meet her soon."

"Trick or treat," the other boy said, and he held out a big paper bag of candy.

I had hardly glanced at the other kid. Now I realized he

was smoking. "If you're old enough to smoke, you are too old to trick-or-treat," I said. I reached out quickly and took his bag from him.

"Hey," he yelled, "you can't do that."

"I told you she's the principal, Joe," said Kash. "Why didn't you get rid of that thing? Besides Coach Pickle could drive by any time, and he'd do a lot more than take your candy."

"Get rid of the cigarette now, Joe," I said, and he did. I held out my hand. "I want the pack too."

He grumbled something I couldn't make out, but he also pulled the package from his shirt pocket and handed them to me. "Good," I said, and I gave him back the bag of candy. I put several little bars into his bag and a whole handful into Kash's. "Do I need to call your parents, Joe?"

"No ma'am," he said.

"Very well, then." I turned toward Kash. "I hope you both enjoy the rest of the evening, and, Kash, I would like to talk to you in my office tomorrow just before the water balloon fight." It was light enough for me to see a disturbed look flash through those wonderful eye. "No problem or anything. I just need your help with something."

With the cigarettes in my hand, I turned back into the living room and closed the door after taking one look at Kash walking away. He was even beautiful from behind. Rendi was still watching TV, but she glanced up at me.

"Bird," she said, "where did you get those things?" I

could see her getting ready to lecture me about the dangers of smoking.

"Let me put them in the trash," I said, and I went into the kitchen to throw them in the can under our sink.

Rendi forgot her movie. I could feel her eyes on my back as I moved. I washed my hands just to drag the time out, but she was still watching for me. "I took them away from a kid who was trick-or-treating, told him he couldn't have candy until he got rid of the cigarettes."

"How old was he?"

"He goes to the middle school," I said, "probably an eighth-grader." I was enjoying this.

Rendi stared at me. "Let me get this straight? You told someone you go to school with that he shouldn't be smoking?"

"I don't know why you're surprised," I said. "Don't you know how bad cigarettes are for you?" I went to my room then. I had to write a speech for the faculty meeting before I could get ready for bed.

Chapter 8

The morning of my last day as principal of Thomas Jefferson Middle School in Prairie Dog Town, Oklahoma, was just as beautiful as the one before. I got up early and packed my backpack with a few things I wanted to take to school. I took my bead curtain down from my door. I could clip it to the inside of the office doorframe. Anyone who opened my door to come in would have to go through the beads first. Sure, I knew I only had one more day, but I wanted to put up some things. I also took my camera. It would be fun to have pictures to send to Katie. I took along a poster of the Twisted Bananas, a group I like a lot. Everyone in the band has hair done up to look like bananas. I stuck in another poster that said, "Maturity Is Overrated" in huge letters and one that had a scene with a girl and guy dressed in clothes from the '60s. It said "Make Love, Not War." I wanted my office to be comfortable even if I did have only one day left. Besides, I would enjoy the look on Mrs. Simpson's face when she saw it all.

I also had a big towel, jeans, and a tee to change into for the water balloon fight—I mean *festival*. I put the bag out on the front porch first thing even though Rendi wasn't up yet. I didn't want to take a chance on her wanting to know what was in the pack.

I dressed in my dark red suit, and I was singing in the kitchen as I took a bowl and cereal from the cabinets. Rendi came wandering in, rubbing her eyes. "It's not even seven. Why are you up?"

"Just couldn't sleep. I thought I'd get to school early, maybe get a chance to meet some people before class."

"They'll let you in the building an hour early?" Rendi looked doubtful, but too sleepy to argue.

"Lots of clubs and things meet before school here," I said. "I'm sure the principal will be there early. She'll let me in. You look tired," I said, "why don't you go back to bed. No need to be up with me."

She looked at me. "Well, I wanted to see you before you went off to say I hope you have a better day than yesterday." She sort of leaned toward me like she wanted a better look or something. "But then I heard you singing. You sounded pretty happy for a girl about to go to a school she hates."

I tried to make my face look long and sad. "Oh, you

● ● ● ● ●

know what they say about singing when it's dark or something to get your courage up."

Rendi sank into a kitchen chair, and I went on with pouring my cereal. "I stepped out on the porch this morning just to check the weather outside. It's beautiful, as warm as summer."

"Indian summer's what people call days like this. Oklahoma has lots of them."

There was something in her voice. "You're glad to be back in Oklahoma, huh?"

"I guess so, but I wish you felt better about being here." She shrugged.

"Don't shrug your shoulders at me," I said in my principal's voice, and we both laughed. I would never have admitted it, but it felt good to laugh with Rendi.

"You have your school supplies?" she asked while I was eating.

"Took them yesterday," I said. "Remember?"

"Oh, yeah." She reached out to touch my cheek. "Why don't you change your clothes, honey? You've got some good jeans and cute shirts."

I shook my head. "No, Rendi. I'll take the other three suits back, but I guess this is sort of a test. If they don't like me because of the way I'm dressed...," I thought for a minute, "Well, kids like that aren't the kinds of kids I want to have as my friends anyway."

"Bird," she said, "that's deep. I'm proud of you, very proud."

"Got to go." I knew Rendi was about to slip into one of her, "let's talk about humanity" moods. I could hear it in her voice.

"Want me to drive you?"

"No, I want to enjoy the walk on this beautiful Indian summer day." I was out the front door before she had a chance to say anything else. I got my backpack and started toward my last hours in the principal's office.

When I got to the big sandstone building, it looked different to me somehow. Maybe the sun was hitting it in a different way. I don't know why, but I liked the looks of the building. I decided to walk around it before I went in so that I could see the spot where the water fight would be.

There was a nice grassy area, and I could just imagine water balloons flying through the air. From behind the school, I could see the gym too. It was a big old building with wide front steps. A girl came up the steps and settled cross-legged on the concrete porch. She took something out of her book bag, and all at once two pigeons came flying down to land beside her. I moved a little closer. I could see then that the girl was tearing off bits of bread to feed the birds, and I could see that the girl was Serenity. I felt sad watching her. I'm telling you the truth, I think I would have known how lonely the girl was just by seeing her with the birds. No one would have had to tell me that Serenity didn't have any people for friends. I knew right then that I'd keep my promise to change that.

I didn't call to Serenity or watch very long. I went back

* * * * *

to the front door, squared my shoulders and got into my principal way of thinking. I got out my key and used it to let myself into the building. I liked having a key to the school, but I supposed they would want it back after my replacement came.

I had the beads and the band poster up and was on a chair tacking up the love one when I heard Mrs. Simpson at her desk. My door was open, so I knew she had already seen the beads. I couldn't wait to show her the rest of my decorations. "Mrs. Simpson," I called, "could you please come in here for a minute?"

I loved seeing her push through the beads. "Do you like what I've done with the place?" I asked. She seemed speechless, so I went on. "I'm thinking of getting some big pillows for the floor. You know, get rid of the chairs. Let my guests make themselves comfortable."

She didn't say anything, just backed out of the beads and closed the door. I didn't hear a peep from her until I walked past her desk on my way to the meeting. "I had the cafeteria send the cinnamon rolls and coffee down to the library," she said. "Everything should be set up by now."

The library had two glass walls just like the outer office, so I had a clear view of the group that waited for me. I clutched the outline of my speech. Last night I had enjoyed writing it, but now seeing real people who would hear me, I felt really nervous. Maybe I should pretend to

• • • • •

get sick suddenly. I had once had a part in a school play where I was an old lady who had a heart attack. I was pretty good with heart attacks, but I decided against it. I'd end up in the hospital and miss the festival.

There were maybe fifteen people in the room, not a big faculty. Most people were already at tables, eating their cinnamon rolls and drinking coffee. A couple of men were still getting their refreshments when I stepped up to the podium. "That's fine, gentlemen," I said with a smile that wasn't genuine. "Get what you need, but I'll go ahead and start the meeting." I paused for a minute. "Think the thought," I told myself. "Well," I said, "here we are, aren't we? I know I didn't get to meet many of you yesterday, but, of course, there were lots of things to take care of on my first day on the job. I know I look young and everything. That's because I am young." I looked at their faces, many of them frowning. "You know," I said, "I may even be the youngest person in this room." I lifted my hands in a sort of helpless gesture. "The thing is, I think the principal's office is making me older fast." I heard a laugh or two and felt encouraged. I went on, "Just wait, maybe I'll catch up with you. The thing I want to do during my very short term as your principal is to concentrate on a serious problem. I want to fight bullying in the school." A few people clapped.

I felt better, but then an angry-looking woman near the front said, "What about this ridiculous water balloon

• • • • •

159

thing the Student Council wants to have? Are you really allowing such a mess?"

"I am," I said, and I think I sounded confident. "I know many of you do not agree with my decision. However, I ask you to remember that my strength is my understanding of young people." I laughed. "In fact, I might be considered one of them." The faces before me did not look friendly. "Let me make you a promise," I said slowly. "I pledge to you that if this water balloon festival does not prove to be a valuable step toward less bullying in this school, I will not be with you tomorrow." I gave them a big nod. "That's right! If the water balloon festival is not a success, I will give up my position."

"Ms. Miller," someone called from the back of the room, but I held up my hand in a sort of stop gesture. "People," I said, "I would like nothing better than to stay here and get to know you all." I pointed toward the clock. "But look at the time." I stepped away from the podium. "Okay, people, go out there and educate!" I pulled up the bottom of my skirt so I could run, and I ran out of the library.

No one followed me. I looked through the glass just as I was even with the corner of the library. Mostly the teachers were standing in little groups, talking. Lots of them were shaking their heads. A few, though, didn't seem interested. They were going back for more cinnamon rolls.

"How'd the meeting go?" Mrs. Simpson said when I came into the office.

"The cinnamon rolls were a big hit." I hurried through the outer office. "I don't want to be disturbed until further notice," I said just before I went through my door. Just to make sure, I flipped the lock.

In Denver, Katie was probably in her mother's SUV on her way to school. I dialed her number. "No party here," she said instead of hello.

I made a face. I didn't like that Katie was now answering her phone with Ivory's pet expression. "Hello, Katie," I said. I tried to emphasize the "hello" so she would get my point that she had not said hello to me.

She didn't get the point. "Bird," she said, "what's happening?"

I couldn't keep the pride out of my voice. "Oh, not much, except that I just held my first faculty meeting."

"Really? You stood up there and talked to a bunch of teachers like you were a regular principal and stuff."

"I did."

"No way! I want to know everything, everything that happened yesterday and everything that happens today."

"I don't have time right now." The wild thing is that just at that very minute, talking on that phone, an idea just came to me, I mean a huge idea. For sure the best idea I'd ever had. "Katie," I said. "A brilliant scheme just flashed through my mind. If I can pull this thing off, you will know everything that's happened, you and a lot of other people. But right now I need that number."

● ● ● ● ●

161

"You mean Marcy Willis's number."

"Yes, you got it for me. Didn't you?"

"Don't break into a sweat. I got it all right. I asked her for it. At first she wouldn't give it to me, thought the Pack wanted it to torment her or something."

"But you got it?"

"Yes, I didn't think she would give it to me if I said you wanted it." There was a little pause. "See, Bird, there's something I kind of forgot to tell you. Since you had moved and everything anyway, Ivory told Mrs. Howard and everyone that you wrote the note. She sort of said you did the whole thing by yourself."

"What?" I pounded my hand on my desk. "The rest of you let her do that? You all went along with it?"

"Well, we didn't see how it could hurt. I mean you were gone and stuff."

I sighed. "Okay, Katie, but did you get the phone number?"

"Yes, finally I told her it was just for me, that I wanted it so I could call her if I had a problem with algebra."

"Well, Katie, you could use some help with algebra. Maybe you ought to call Marcy sometime."

There was silence on Katie's end for a minute. Then she said, "Bird, you know Ivory wouldn't like it if I called Marcy. The Six-Pack has rules about talking to girls like her."

"Katie," I said, "give me the number."

"Okay, hold on. I've got it written in my algebra book."

* * * * *

"Good place for it," I said, then Katie repeated the number, and I wrote it down. "Thanks, Katie. Most of the time you're a real friend, and I'm glad I got a chance to know you."

She made a surprised sound with her breath. "Bird, don't talk like that. I mean, you sound like we might never talk again. You still think you will come back to Denver, don't you? When you do, we will drop the new girl from the Six-Pack. Anyway, I think Ivory will agree to that."

"I don't know if we will come back or not, but, Katie, I want to tell you something. I'm pretty sure that once you've been a principal, you can't be in the Six-Pack ever again. It just wouldn't work."

"I don't understand you anymore, Bird."

"That's okay," I said. "Lots of other people feel the same way."

After the phone call, I couldn't think about anything except my idea. I didn't want to start on it, though, until after the balloon fight. I needed something to help me calm down. I picked up my bag and got out the book Ivory had insisted I carry out from the library. I'd send it back, but before I did, I'd read it. It looked interesting. I read for a long time, until Mrs. Simpson buzzed me.

"I know you said no disturbances, but Coach Pickle is here with popcorn. He is insisting you would want to see him."

I looked up at the clock. It was almost eleven, time for *All My Secrets.* "Yes, send him in," I told her.

"I used the popcorn machine down in the concession stand we have in the gym." He handed me a nice warm bag, set the other bag on my desk, and took two colas from the bag he had across his shoulder. "We'll just power back after a hard morning, and take a little break. Don't worry about spoiling your lunch. Today is spaghetti day in the cafeteria, horrible stuff."

We really got into the program, and when *Secrets* was over, we started on *Specific Hospital.* Coach Pickle filled me in on background. In the first scene, Lorraine was in a hospital bed, near death. She had divorced Carl years earlier and been married to five or six other men, but now she realized she had always loved Carl, who happens to be her doctor. "My life has been empty without you, my love, if only I had realized while I had time left to spend with you," she said. Carl told her that he was going to perform an experimental surgery on her, but that her chances were slim.

Coach Pickle was sniffing. I handed him a tissue. He's got a soft heart, I thought. Maybe Rendi would like to date him. She had certainly done worse. I was pretty sure Richard, whose picture was still in my bag, didn't have a tender heart. Just then Mrs. Simpson buzzed. "Teachers in the cafeteria are asking for you. Word is that there will be a spaghetti fight today to protest the food."

"I'll take care of it," I said.

Of course, Coach Pickle heard Mrs. Simpson's message. "Do you want me to come with you?" he said.

"No." I patted his shoulder as I walked by. "You stay right here, power back. You deserve a rest. I think I can handle this."

Just as I walked into the cafeteria, two boys, a table apart, picked up several strings of spaghetti and threw them at each other. "Stop this at once," I shouted. Then I scooted over a kid's plate, held up my skirt, and climbed on a table. I noticed that several of the kids had picked up pieces of spaghetti too, but they put them down when I yelled. "Listen to me," I said, "I understand you do not like what you've been served today."

"No." Their shouted answer filled the room.

I looked down and saw for the first time that Kash Edge sat at the table I stood on. Kash looked so hot in a gold-colored tee that I almost forgot why I was standing on a cafeteria table. I forced my mind back to the food. "I'll taste the spaghetti, and let you know what I think." I pointed to Kash. "Young man, would you mind handing up a bite from your plate?"

He stood up and held out his fork wrapped with spaghetti. I felt a thrill pass through my hand and up my arm when I took the fork. But I made myself concentrate on the food. The room was totally silent as I chewed. I made a face. "Terrible," I said, and the entire student body cheered. The cooks had stepped out of the kitchen, and they stood with their arms folded, staring up at me.

"Is one of you Doris Davis?" I asked.

A large, angry-looking woman stepped forward. "That would be me." She glared at me.

"Mrs. Davis, I understand you are the head of this cafeteria," I said. She nodded, and I went on. "First, let me say that I have never tasted better cinnamon rolls than the ones you bake."

"Thank you," she said, and she almost smiled at me.

"Next, let me say your spaghetti . . . Well, shall we say your spaghetti needs work. I don't want you to be here tomorrow. I want you to spend the day with Judy at City Café. I will arrange for her to give you lessons on making spaghetti. Your staff can serve cold cuts in your absence. What do you think?"

"Reckon that would be all right with me. Don't think there's shame in needing to learn."

"Excellent," I said. "I'll call Judy, and by the way, I want you to take Thursday off too. Sort of a thank-you from the principal's office."

The kids all cheered again, and I noticed that some of the cooks were clapping too. "Young man," I said to Kash, who was still standing near me, "would you help me down?"

He put up his hand. I took it, and this time the tingle went through my entire body. "I'll call for you just before last hour," I said softly when I was beside him.

. . . . .

I went back to my office, closed the door, and read most of the afternoon. At two, I buzzed Mrs. Simpson. "I want to see the Edge boy," I said. "I believe his name is Kash, is that right?"

"Yes, Kash. He's a very nice boy."

"I'm sure he is," I said. "Please have him sent down here at once."

When he came into my office, I could hardly keep from making a whistling sound because he looked so hot. The sleeves of his shirt were rolled up so that the top of those beautiful arms showed. I had pulled the chair from the other side of the desk to make it closer to me. "Sit down, please," I said, and I put my hands in my lap. I was afraid if I didn't fasten them together, I would lose control and reach out to touch him.

"Did you find a note in your bike basket?" I asked.

"Yes." He looked down at the floor.

"I imagine you found the note somewhat confusing."

"I sure did. It said I had an admirer, but it was written on a pad that said from the principal's office."

"Well, I promise you will understand everything before you leave here, but first I need to talk to you about one of your classmates who is a very troubled girl. Her name is Serenity Blair. You know her, don't you?"

"Sure," he said, and he looked up at me for a second before dropping his eyes again. "Prairie Dog Town is awful small, Ms. Miller. Everyone knows everyone else."

"Have you noticed that Serenity is tormented by some of the other kids?"

"I guess I have."

"She tells me that a certain group of girls started it, and others follow."

"Chicken fever," said Kash, and he nodded his head like he wanted to agree with himself.

I wasn't sure I had understood him. "Chicken fever?"

"Yes, ma'am. Don't you know what that is?"

This time I didn't even pretend to have any knowledge of what he was talking about. "No, tell me about it."

"Well," he said, "my grandparents own a farm out west of town. I spend lots of time out there, and I've seen chicken fever. Two baby chickens get in a fight, pecking at each other. One makes the other bleed. If you don't get that little chicken out of the pen, the others will all turn on it, peck it to death." He shrugged. "Don't know why, but anyway, some kids are like that. They see that someone is getting pecked on. They see the blood, and they start to peck too."

"You're right," I said, "and you are a very intelligent boy." I wanted to say handsome too, intelligent and awesomely handsome. "Would you like to help me put a stop to chicken fever in the eighth grade?"

He looked at me for a minute, thinking. Then he nodded his head. "Always have hated to find a little chicken dead and bleeding. What can I do?"

I told him that Serenity feared the water balloon fight because she knew Nicole and her group would turn on her. "I want to be ready to step in when they do."

"You're going to tell them to stop?"

"No," I said, "I want to bombard them with balloons, show them how it feels. The thing is, though, I may need help."

His eyebrows wrinkled with worry. "I'd feel sort of funny hitting girls and all, if that's what you mean, especially Nicole."

A cold feeling started around my heart. "Why especially Nicole?"

"Remember yesterday how I told you I'd just called it quits with a girl?" I nodded, and he went on. "Well, Nicole is the girl. I don't know." He shrugged. "It would just feel funny hitting her like that."

I stood up. "I understand," I said, and I hoped my voice didn't feel as sad as I felt. "You may go now, Kash."

He got up slowly. "I could tell Hannah and Julie and maybe some of the other girls on Student Council to be ready to help you."

"Thank you," I said.

Kash was standing up now, but he didn't move toward the door. "Ms. Miller," he said, "you were going to explain about the note."

I swallowed hard. I couldn't tell him now that I had written the note. I didn't feel like telling him that I wasn't

* * * * *

the principal either. He could find it out with all the others, with his girlfriend Nicole. "Oh," I said. "I saw the girl who put the note in your basket. In fact, she stopped at my car to borrow the piece of paper." I sighed. "I've decided, though, not to tell you who she is. I don't think you could be interested in her. She has a really long neck."

"I'm not much interested in having a new girlfriend right now anyway," he said, then he grinned. "Can't think of any girl in our school who has a long neck, though." He looked at me, and for a minute I thought his eyes went to my neck.

When he left, I just sat at my desk and fought tears. Kash still had feelings for Nicole. I wondered why he broke up with her. It didn't make sense, but things like that happened. For instance, there was Lorraine and Carl, on *Specific Hospital*. I was so lost in thought that I had not noticed that Kash left the door open, or that Mrs. Simpson had come to push back the beads and stand in the doorway. "You look very sad," she said. "Dare I hope you have decided to call off the water balloon thing and now you are dreading to tell the students?"

"No, the festival will go on. I am feeling down because Kash Edge doesn't like me."

"I know you don't like for me to give you advice, dear, and I am fully aware that you have had a great many education courses. Still, I have to say this. Being well liked by the students should not be the goal of an administrator or teacher. Believe me, I've been around here long enough to have seen plenty and to have learned a thing or two. It really doesn't matter whether Kash Edge or any other student likes you. What you want is respect."

I made myself smile. "Well, I think he does respect me, or at least he will when he sees how good I am at throwing water balloons. I've got to get ready now."

"God help us," Mrs. Simpson said, and she closed the door.

First I took my principal's pad and wrote my confession note. "Dear New Principal, My name is Robin Miller, just like yours. That's why I got to be principal here for two days instead of being a new girl in eighth grade. It was a huge amount of fun, and I learned a lot. You will find that the spaghetti is better in the cafeteria now, and I hope there will be less bullying in the eighth grade. I hope you will agree that those improvements aren't bad for just two days in this office. I have one bit of advice for you about Mrs. Simpson. She is a nice person, but don't let her tell you what to do. I think you will like this school. I imagine I will be one of the first students you have to punish, so I guess we will meet soon. Most sincerely, Robin (BTW, call me 'Bird') Miller." I reread the note and was pleased with it. I did write, "P.S. If you need help, I recommend Madam Zelda at the Psychic Emergency Line."

Next I locked my office door, stripped off the suit, and put on my jeans, a big T-shirt, and my sneakers. I opened the closet because I had seen a mirror on the door. I let down my hair from the knot and brushed it. Then I put it up in a pony tail. Next I touched up my lipstick. When I was finished, I looked at myself for a long time. "Where have you been, Bird?" I asked out loud. "You've waited long enough. It is time for the students of Thomas Jefferson Middle School to meet you."

The Student Council kids had a long table set up, and it was already filled with balloons. They also had rolls of blue tickets. "Each kid gets four tickets," Hannah told me. "Tickets can be exchanged for water balloons. We don't want any one person to hog them, you know." She pointed toward her right where several red wagons stood. They were full of more balloons. "Student Council members will deliver more ammunition in exchange for tickets."

A man with a camera and a notepad was running around talking to people. Hannah told me he was a reporter from the newspaper over in Ponca City. "I called them," she said. "I think we should be in the paper, since it's the coolest thing the Student Council has ever done."

The man came over to take my picture with Hannah. "The principal and the student organizer," he said before he pushed the button. "I don't think anyone could guess which is older, not by looks."

"Getting the newspaper was good thinking, Hannah," I said when the photographer was finished. "You've done a great job." I started to walk away, but Hannah wasn't finished.

"Oh, Ms. Miller, wait. I have something I want to tell you."

I turned back to her. "Okay."

"Dennis sinned," she said, and she smiled.

"And who is Dennis?"

She didn't answer just asked, "Do geese see God?"

I put my hand on her shoulder. "Hannah, you are certainly into theological issues today."

"Huh?"

"*Theological,* means having to do with God, religion, stuff like that."

She laughed. "No," she said. "They're palindromes. 'Dennis sinned', and 'do geese see God' are the same backward as forward."

"You're right, Hannah. Maybe after this water balloon festival, you should talk to the principal about trying for the palindrome record."

Hannah smiled. "I'll come into the office to talk to you about it. You are just the coolest principal ever."

"I certainly hope the principal of this school will always be cool." The school door opened. "Look," I said. "Here come our fighters."

As the kids came out, Coach Pickle organized them into two sides. From the numbers, I figured there weren't many in the library doing research on global warming.

Serenity was near the end of her line. I noticed that Nicole, Katelin, Caitlyn, and Ashley (all wearing their purple jackets) had piles of balloons. I could see them watching Serenity, who brought her balloons over to stand not far from me. I took a few balloons myself. When the last kid had ammunition, Coach Pickle blew his whistle. "All right, people, we expect you to play fair. Prairie Dogs always do." I saw the Purples laughing. The coach was still talking. "No one should be hit in the neck, face, or head. Come out throwing," he yelled.

Right off I felt a balloon hit me between the shoulders. I whirled around. Mrs. Simpson had come out the door. There were no balloons in her hands. She waved at me. I was trying to decide whether she had thrown them at me, when I heard Serenity yell. As I turned, two balloons smashed into her chest. One at a time, I hurled my balloons at Nicole.

I wished for more ammunition, but balloons from somewhere were hitting the purple coats. Then I saw them. Hannah and four girls I didn't know were behind the Purples, and they were throwing balloon after balloon at them. Then I saw something that made me jump up and shout, "Yes!"

Kash was behind Hannah, hunkered down beside a red wagon full of balloons, and he handed them off quickly to Hannah and her friends.

"Stop it!" yelled Nicole. "None of you are following the rules. Kash Edge, you are helping them be mean."

I opened my mouth to interfere, but Kash could take care of himself. "We're not being mean." He stood up and walked closer to the Purples. "We're the people who make sure no one gets picked on."

"I am not picking on anyone." Nicole's voice sounded near tears. "We're just having fun with Serenity, just girl stuff. You don't understand. That's all." She turned her back. "Come on," she said to the other Purples. "Let's get out of here."

Just then Coach Pickle yelled, "Game's over. You did a good job of following the rules. Get your towels and dry off. Bell's about to ring."

"Coach," I shouted. "I have one announcement." I walked over to the Student Council table and climbed on it. "Prairie Dogs!" I yelled. "The weatherman says tomorrow may be our last day of Indian summer. Let's meet the sun with skin! No dress code for tomorrow. Wear short shorts, crop tops, let those midriffs show, tank tops, muscles shirts, no rules!" The crowd cheered. I stood on that table and looked out at the Prairie Dogs, and I knew I was having my last look at them as their principal.

I climbed down and looked around for Kash, but I couldn't see him in the group of wet kids who were hurrying toward the school door. I would have to wait to tell him who I was and who had written the note.

I made my way back to the office. Mrs. Simpson was at her desk. "Well," she said, "I have to say it wasn't as bad as

• • • • •

I expected. I can see why the kids enjoyed it so much." She had a little smile around her lips, and I was pretty sure she had thrown the balloon at me.

I smiled back at her. "I'll be in my office for a while. Please see that no one disturbs me. After I change my clothes, I have a very important phone call to make." All the time I dried and dressed, I planned what I would say on the phone. When I was dressed, I took the phone, asked for a number in Chicago, and made the call that would change all our lives.

Chapter 9

Here is what happened later, and I've pretty much put it all in order as far as when it happened. I called Marcy Willis, and I told her that I was sorry. At first she thought it was a trick of some kind, but before I hung up, she knew I was serious.

I confessed all about being principal to Rendi, who tried to act like she thought what I did was terrible, but who couldn't carry off the part about being mad at me because she was so proud of the part about me helping Serenity.

I went to school Wednesday thinking the new principal might make me roadkill. "Just sit over there," Mrs. Simpson said when I came into the office. "The *principal*" (she gave me a hard look) "is on the phone with the superintendent. They are deciding what to do with you. We don't like being lied to around here."

I couldn't say I was sorry for what I had done. I mean it was a great amount of fun and besides, I really learned a lot. I could see, though, that Mrs. Simpson resented being fooled by a kid, and I honestly did feel bad about that.

"You were so nice to me," I said, almost whispering. "I'm sorry if I hurt your feelings."

She looked up at me. Her eyes were cold at first, but then they changed, and a little grin started around her mouth. "Well," she said. "I did hit you with a water balloon. We'll call it even. You won't get off so easily in there, though." She leaned her head toward the principal's office.

I went over to sit down, and after what seemed like a long time, Ms. Miller came to the door to call me into her office. She was a pretty woman, dressed very stylishly in gaucho pants with boots. Her neck was the perfect length too. I figured even Angie Bradford would have to approve of her looks. "I have your beads and things." She pointed to a box with my stuff in it. "I'll give them back to you if we don't need to hold them for evidence."

I swallowed hard. Did she mean there would be a regular trial with a judge and everything? "You may sit down." I took the chair beside the door, and I wondered how long I would have to sit there.

Right off she wanted to know why I would do such a thing. I tried to think of some good-sounding reason, but I couldn't. "Well, it wasn't premeditated or anything." I knew people got in less trouble for crimes if they weren't planned.

"I guess when I got the chance . . . I mean Mrs. Simpson told me to come right into my office." I shrugged. "I guess the temptation was just too great."

Ms. Miller told me that some of the teachers had asked her not to be too hard on me. That's when she smiled at me for the first time. "I think Coach Pickle is disappointed that you won't be his boss," she said, but then she brought up Madam Zelda.

I confessed that I knew the phone bill was going to be pretty bad, and Ms. Miller said I would have to pay it. I thought I would ask my grandparents for the money, but Ms. Miller said I should have to work for it. She called Rendi, who called Judy, and they all decided that I could work in the café after school until my bill was paid.

I did not tell Ms. Miller about the phone call I had made to Chicago, because nothing was definite yet. When I first called, it seemed like no one would talk to me, but then I got hold of the right person and got listened to. Still, the people in Chicago had to have a meeting or something and then if they decided to "explore the possibility further" (their words), they would call the school to verify that I hadn't made the whole story up. I thought it would be best if the people in Chicago told Ms. Miller my stupendous idea.

I left the office knowing I had lots of detention to do and lots of work as a waitress in front of me. All over the building that day you could see a lot of skin. I mean they couldn't make everyone go home and change could they? When I went into second period English class (I didn't make it to first period because of all the waiting and discussing in the office), all the kids stood up and cheered, even Nicole. Mrs. Hoover, the teacher, asked me where I wanted to sit, and I was thrilled because there was an empty seat right behind Kash Edge, but I was disappointed because he didn't mention the note. I mean, I was pretty sure he had figured out by that time that I wrote the note, don't you think?

The *Opal* show came to Thomas Jefferson Middle School in Prairie Dog Town, Oklahoma! Yes! You heard me. That was the phone call to Chicago. I called up the producers of the show and told them my story. I told them everything, all about Denver and the Six-Pack and Marcy and the slight misunderstanding that made me the principal and about Serenity and the Purples. BTW, I guess I didn't really tell them everything because I did not mention Kash Edge. I mean what could I say except that he obviously was not interested in being my boyfriend and that at first I thought it was because of Nicole, but it wasn't, so then I was pretty sure it was because of my long neck. The producers had to talk before they called the new principal, but I think I told you that, and I don't want to go repeating myself and stuff. Anyway, by noon, we knew the show was coming, and everyone thought that was so cool and they seemed to think I was cool too.

• • • • •

On the day before the show was filmed, I woke up really excited. I guess everyone in the whole town of Prairie Dog Town (which of course is not a huge amount of people) woke up excited too. I mean, everyone knew Opal would be coming to our town tomorrow. The filming would take place in the gym, where a temporary stage was being built on one end of the basketball court.

I had talked to the producers plenty, and they had spent lots of time with Coach Pickle getting stuff ready in the gym. On that morning before the show, I woke up knowing I would see Ivory and Katie again. At first I thought the show was going to bring all five remaining members of the Six-Pack, but then they decided to leave off Felicity, Taylor, and Stephanie because that would be too many to interview. I was glad. I mean, it would be hard enough to face Ivory without her followers to give her strength.

They were being flown into Oklahoma City, where they would be met by one of the TV producers who would bring them to Prairie Dog Town. Mrs. Morford, Katie's mother, was coming with them. So was Marcy Willis. They would be staying at a motel in Ponca City, but the producer would bring them to our school just about the time school was out for the day.

The Denver girls were going to be the guests of our school for a big pizza party and dance in the gym after school. My favorite of the *Opal* team was Shan, a cool

* * * * *

woman with the most beautiful straight black hair. She wore it twisted and hanging down her back. She liked me too. I could tell she wasn't just being nice to me because it was her job and stuff. Shan called me at home before I left for school that morning. "Great news, Bird, I am going to the airport in Oklahoma City with a cameraman to get shots of the kids as they come off the plane. I have permission to take you to Oklahoma City with me so you can meet your friends and ride back here with them. We just need to make sure your mother is cool with that."

I twisted my face into all sort of contortions and tried to think what I wanted to do. I knew it would be a blast to ride with Shan. We would talk heart-to-heart all the way, and she would tell me more funny stories about things that have happened on the show. The thing was, though, if I went I would be standing there in the airport when the girls came walking off the plane.

I didn't mind seeing Marcy because we'd made our peace, and I would be glad to see Katie. Ivory, that was completely different. Oh, sure I knew she had mixed feelings. I mean it was exciting to get out of school and go flying off to be on the *Opal* show. Shan had told me that Ivory told everyone she had learned her lesson. None of that fooled me. I knew Ivory had to resent what I had done too, and Ivory always made people pay.

"Bird?" Shan said into the phone. "Are you there? What do you think?"

"Oh," I said. "Thanks a lot. That would be a lot of fun, but, you know what, I really need to be in English class today. We are all doing research papers, and I got off to a late start. I guess I'd better stay here."

"Bird," said Shan, "is there something else going on here besides a research paper? Is there something we need to talk about?"

"No," I lied. "I'm just worried about getting my paper done." I told her good-bye and hung up, feeling like a coward for being afraid to face Ivory. I guess you can figure out that I didn't accomplish much on my paper or anything else that day.

Serenity was excited about getting the works from the hair and makeup people before the show the next day. At lunch the two of us mostly talked about what we would wear and how we would have our hair done. Of course, I kept my eye on Kash, who ate with a group of boys at the next table. Principal Miller called the eighth grade into the cafeteria during last hour to talk to us about how to act at the party. She stood up in front of us and held up her hand until we were perfectly quiet. "There will be TV cameras there, people," she said, and she moved her head, looking into all of our faces. "Don't do anything to make your parents or your school ashamed of you."

Nicole walked beside me as we left the cafeteria. "We aren't even wearing our jackets to the party," she told me. "I mean they told us to wear them on the show tomorrow, and it's not like we are giving up the group or anything." She reached out and squeezed my arm. "Tonight, though, we just want everyone to consider themselves purple."

"That's amazing," I said, and I smiled at her like what I said was a compliment. I knew Nicole and I would be butting heads in the future, but for a few days, I just wanted peace.

The eighth-graders, all thirty of us, were in the gym when the girls from Denver came in. Ivory walked in front of Katie, and Ivory had her arm looped through Marcy Willis's like Marcy was just the most important person in the world to her. "Oh, gag," I said, but no one heard me because Principal Miller and Coach Pickle were up on the stage. She was clapping while he cheered and made motions for us to cheer too.

What happened next really amazed me. I made my way up to the stage because Principal Miller had asked me to be up there when the girls introduced themselves to our class. Coach Pickle handed me the microphone. "These are my friends from Denver," I said, but I felt funny saying it. Katie was my friend and now maybe Marcy, but I knew Ivory wasn't. One at a time the girls took the mike and said their names.

"Let's give them all a big Prairie Dog welcome," said Coach Pickle, and the kids clapped again. "All right," said the coach. "Fill up on pizza and dance, dance, dance."

• • • • •

I went down the steps with the Denver girls right be-hind me. Everybody hugged me. "You look taller," Ivory said. She stepped back from me to sort of study me. "No, maybe not taller, maybe it's just that your . . ." She stopped like she had just caught herself, but, of course, I knew she was doing it on purpose.

"Were you going to say my neck is longer?" I shook my head. "I hope so. In Oklahoma a woman with a long neck is considered beautiful. You know, like stretched out lips are in some African tribes? We actually have a machine here in the gym for girls to stretch their necks on."

Ivory stared at me, but then she laughed and put her hand on my shoulder. "Bird, you're wicked! For just a minute I believed you!"

Katie was standing right beside me and we were talk-ing when I heard, "My name is Kash. Would you like to dance?" For a minute I thought he was talking to me, but, of course, I knew his name. I saw he was looking at Katie. Ivory knew who he meant too, but she acted like she didn't. I'm telling you the truth. She jumped in front of Katie, took Kash's hand, and walked off with him.

I almost died right there on the gym floor. Another boy came over and asked Katie to dance, and then a guy asked Marcy. This was weird. At all the dances I'd been to in Denver, the boys stood in one group and the girls in an-other. They looked at each other for a long time before a few brave boys asked someone to dance. But Prairie Dog

* * * * *

Town was different, and there was Ivory dancing away with the boy I loved.

I stumbled out of the way, and Serenity found me leaning against a wall. "Don't worry," she said.

"About what?"

"About Kash dancing with that Ivory girl. I heard Coach Pickle tell the boys he'd make them run a zillion extra laps in gym if they didn't pay special attention to the visiting girls and stuff."

I had never said a word to Serenity about liking Kash. "What makes you think I care what Kash Edge does?"

She laughed. "Come off it, Bird! Like you aren't watching him every minute!"

"Let's get some pizza," I said.

Serenity wanted to take some of her pizza out to her pigeons, and I went along. Feeding Winston and Churchill was certainly better than watching the dancers. We sat on the steps, and the birds came right up to eat out of Serenity's hand. "You know Coach Pickle would have a fit if he saw you feeding those birds. He doesn't want them hanging around the gym."

"You don't have to be the principal anymore, remember?" She tore more pizza into little pieces and held them out to the birds. "Coach Pickle is too busy making boys dance to worry about two little birds right now. Just think, tomorrow Opal Gentry will be right here in Prairie Dog Town, and we will be talking to her. How many people will be watching, do you think?"

* * * * *

"I don't know, but I'll ask Shan." I sighed. "I'm wondering if Richard will be watching." (I had told Serenity about my father, even showed her the picture, but I guess she didn't remember his name.)

"Who's Richard?"

"My father, remember? I mean, I know most of the audience will be women, but if he is still painting he might have a TV in his studio."

"Are you hoping he will call you?"

I shrugged. "I guess. Let's go back inside." The pigeons followed us to the door, but we shooed them away. Inside, the music had changed to a slow song. The two other Prairie Dog Town boys had left their Denver partners, but Kash hadn't. Five or six couples danced in the center of the floor, and there were Kash and Ivory right in the middle of them. She had her hands locked behind his head. His hands were on her waist, and they moved slowly together.

Katie and Marcy sat in folding chairs near a wall, and we went over to join them. "It's my fault about Ivory and Kash," said Katie, and she looked down at her shoes.

I reached over to wave my hand in front of her face until she looked up. "How could it be your fault?"

"I told the Pack all about him, his name and everything." She frowned. "You know Ivory. When she hears about someone having anything, a boyfriend or a new purse. She takes it as a challenge."

"Well," I said, "to be fair, Kash Edge couldn't exactly be

* * * * *

187

called my boyfriend, but, yes, I do know Ivory. I'm just wondering why I was so stupid, letting her tell me what to wear and who to talk to." Katie looked uncomfortable. "I'm not blaming you for still being part of the Pack. I know how hard it would be to stand up to Ivory."

"But Ivory seems lots better," said Marcy. "She's been real nice to me on this trip."

"She'll be nice on the show tomorrow too," I said, "but I wouldn't count on her niceness holding out too long after the cameras are off.

We danced after that, just moving to the music and having a good time even though we didn't have partners. Then Joe, the cigarette-smoking trick-or-treater, came over to stand beside me.

"Hey," he said, "if I promise I haven't been smoking, will you dance with me?" I tried to concentrate on the music, not looking at Kash and Ivory, but it was really hard. I was glad when the party was finally over.

I was telling Katie good night when Ivory came up to hug me. "Oh, Bird," she said. "Thank you for thinking up this *Opal* thing. It is so much fun, and meeting Kash makes it all so awesome." I wandered outside and left Katie with Ivory.

Rendi picked me up, and I was quiet on the way home. "Is something wrong, honey?" she asked.

"Just tired." I rested against the seat.

"Were you glad to see your friends again?"

• • • • •

"Yes, especially Katie, and you know what? I talked some at the party with Marcy Willis. She's okay."

"Good. Anything else you want to tell me?"

"That's all."

"Well tomorrow's the big day."

"Uh-huh," I said.

When we got home, I went straight to bed, but I didn't go to sleep for a long time. My bed is beside the window. I pushed back the curtain and looked out at the night. There was a full moon. I remembered a song Rendi used to sing to me about seeing the moon. One line went, "Let the moon that shines on me shine on the one I love." I wondered if Kash might be looking at the moon. Well, if he was, I was sure he was thinking about Ivory.

In the morning, one of the dressing rooms in the gym was turned into a place for hair and makeup people to work on all of us who were going to be on the show. I couldn't see myself in the mirror as they worked on me, and I was totally surprised when I looked. My hair was all soft around my face, and my eyes were shining. "You look lovely," said the woman who had worked on me.

Someone had been working on Kash too. I wondered why they thought they could improve on how he looked. When I saw that he had been watching while I had my hair done, I wanted to slide down in my chair and wait for him to go away. He didn't leave, though, just stood there and smiled.

• • • • •

I pulled in a deep breath and got the nerve to speak to him. "What's up?" I asked.

He shrugged. "They're working on Ivory, and I'm enjoying a little break without her."

"Huh?" I didn't even try to hide my amazement. "I thought you two were . . . ," I made a face, "you know . . . together."

He shook his head. "She latched on to me. Stuck tight. I didn't know what to do. I mean Coach said be nice, and I figured she'd be going home today, so it didn't matter so much until I found out about the note."

"The note?"

"Yeah, the one on the principal's pad." He grinned at me, and stuck his hands in his pockets.

"You know who wrote the note, don't you?" I asked.

"I do now. Serenity just told me this morning. Until then, I thought it was her. I mean she came in the store that day, and you said someone had just borrowed paper from you. Serenity's okay, but . . ." He just stood there grinning at me.

"So?"

"Well, I don't want to get married or anything, but do you want to sort of hang out with me?"

"I do," I said, and I wanted to dance around the dressing room.

By the time for the show to begin, the gym was full. I had two surprises. Miss Deirdre sent me a dozen roses and a note that said, "To my Star," and my grandparents showed up!

I didn't know that Rendi had called them, but they came to the dressing room with her to see me just before the show. "You look beautiful," said my grandfather.

"And we are so proud of how you are standing up for kids who need it." Grandma slipped her arm through Rendi's. "Your mother brought you up right."

TV sets on big shelves on both sides of the stage let us see what the cameras were filming. The show started with Opal's voice saying. "Today we have an amazing story for you, the story of how a girl who came to a new school to enroll in the eighth grade ended up running the school for two days. We are interested in how this fourteen-year-old carried off her job as principal, but we are even more interested in what she learned about a problem, a disease, really, that runs rampant in our schools. We are talking about bullying, kids picking on kids." Opal came out then from behind a curtain, and she sat down on a chair. The kids, Ivory, Marcy, Katie, Nicole, Serenity, Kash, and me, were all on two sofas on either side of Opal's chair. Kash sat between me and Nicole. Serenity was on our sofa too. The Denver girls were on the other side. I watched the TV set while Opal talked on about how my mother had taken me out of school for picking on a girl. She also told how I ended up being confused with the interim principal because we had the same name, and she told the audience that I use the name Bird. She said that I was an amazing actress. Yes, she did! Shan stood down in front of me, and she lifted her arm when it was time for me to quit watching the monitor and look at Opal because the camera was on me.

"I understand you almost had your mother arrested, Bird." The camera went out to Rendi in the front row of the audience. I knew that would happen, so while I explained about the kidnapping episode, I could watch the TV. Rendi looked pretty and happy sitting by my grandparents. I hoped this might be a sort of fresh start in their relationship. It crossed my mind that I might try just plain telling my mother and my grandmother that I wanted them to get along.

Next the camera went to the girls from Denver. Opal asked all three of them questions. Marcy talked about what we had done to her, and Katie and Ivory both said they were sorry. "I've learned so much from this experience," said Ivory. "I'll never be the same girl again. I've even met a wonderful boy."

That last sentence was a surprise. Ivory hadn't mentioned that during the rehearsal. I saw Shan shake her head no, and Opal went right on, ignoring the part about the boy.

"Did you enjoy being the principal, Bird?" Opal asked.

I talked about watching TV in the office and about calling the Psychic Emergency Line for help and how I was working at Judy's café to pay the bill. People laughed

• • • • •

when I mentioned Madam Zelda, and I hoped she was not watching.

"So, Bird," said Opal, "I know you called Marcy to apologize for your part in tormenting her. What made you do that?"

"I met Serenity. She was sent to my office for slapping someone who was picking on her, and after talking to her, I started to see things from a different point of view." I was nervous, and I wished I could be playing a part. Being Bird Miller was a hard role. I was glad to get the signal that the camera was on Serenity, who talked about how I had given her the necklace and promised she would have a friend. She explained about the Purples too, and next Nicole swore that she too had learned her lesson.

The camera moved to Kash after Opal said, "A young man got involved in this problem, and he was willing to take a stand." She asked Kash to explain chicken fever, and he also talked about how I had asked him to help. Then it was time for a surprise from Opal. "You're a cutie-pie," she said when Kash had finished talking. "Do you have a girlfriend?" That part hadn't been rehearsed. Kash's face turned red, and for just a second he ducked his head. Then he reached over, took my hand, and raised our hands together. "Well, sort of," he said. The audience laughed again.

I looked over at Ivory, who looked so mad I expected smoke to come out of her ears. She jumped up, crossed her arms, and stomped the floor. Shan motioned wildly for Ivory to sit down. The camera was still on Opal, who was talking about how some kids are so angry and hurt inside that they want to hurt other people. She explained that other kids too often just let the bullying go on, sometimes out of fear of being picked on themselves.

I saw the pigeon right off, but at first I didn't think about it flying straight to the stage. Winston or Churchill (I didn't know which) must have known Serenity was up there, though, because that is where he headed.

"My lands," said Opal. "There's a bird in here." The camera went to the bird just as it dropped its load on Ivory's head. "Oh my!" said Opal. "We'll get this child cleaned up." I had to put my hand over my mouth to stop my laughing.

The show ended with us kids standing across the stage holding hands. Ivory was back for the last scene, but I could see that the front of her hair was wet. The camera came to a close-up of me. "We want to challenge kids everywhere to take a stand with us against bullying," I said, and then I remembered something else I hadn't practiced, but wanted to add. "And we are against global warming too," I added.

"Bird," said Opal right at the end, "some special friends of your family told us your mother is in need of work." The camera flashed on Sheriff Walters and Judy in the audience. "And we want this town to have something to remember us by." Opal went on to announce how she had arranged for a grant that would commission Rendi to make a giant prairie dog for the town square, and she talked about what would be on the show next time.

Opal left right away, and it didn't take long for the crew to pack up. Shan was driving the girls and Mrs. Morford back to Oklahoma City to catch a plane. Katie and Marcy hugged me when I said good-bye, but Ivory didn't look at me. I hoped she really had learned a lesson, but I didn't have any faith that even a pigeon could teach Ivory much.

I stood watching the car drive away, and I was glad I was staying in Prairie Dog Town. Rendi was out there with me, and when I turned back from watching the car, Coach Pickle had come up to talk to her. I wondered what they might be talking about.

So the whole thing had this kind of fairy-tale ending, don't you think? I mean with the wicked witch (Ivory) being punished (by pigeons) and the often misunderstood, but brave, girl (me) getting the prince (you totally know who he is).

Oh yes, I bet you expect me to tell about how Richard called me after he saw the show. Not! I quit carrying his picture with me and put it away in a drawer. I got it out, though, five days later.

On the first Saturday after Opal's show, Rendi and I went to Tulsa to spend the weekend. Grandma had asked us right after we finished taping the show, and I said yes without even giving Rendi a chance to speak. She didn't contradict me, though.

We were driving toward Tulsa on the Cimarron Turnpike when I decided to tell Rendi right out how I felt. "I think you ought to work on getting along with Grandma," I said. "How would you feel if I grew up and never came around you or anything?"

Rendi was quiet at first, like maybe she hadn't heard me, but of course I knew she had. Finally she said very softly, "It would break my heart."

"Well?" I answered. Rendi didn't say anything else, but all that weekend I could see she was trying. We went shopping at this very nice shopping center called Utica Square, where there were all kinds of neat stores.

"Could I buy you both outfits?" Grandma asked.

For an instant I saw Rendi stiffen, and I was afraid she would make some comment about Grandma not thinking she dressed decently. I reached out real quick like, took Rendi's hand, and squeezed it. "That would be nice, Mom," she said.

We ended up both buying pants, boots, and sweaters. They weren't alike or anything. That would have looked dumb. I thought the new clothes made us look really cool. Grandma was pleased. "Take their pictures, Horace," she told Grandpa when we were back at the house.

Rendi and I stood in front of the fireplace, and Grandpa was about to push the button when Rendi called, "Wait."

She held out her hand to Grandma. "Come stand with us," she said, and Grandma did.

"All three of my girls together," said Grandpa. Then he took the picture.

Rendi wore her new outfit the next weekend. On Thursday evening, she was working in her studio when the phone rang. I was still hoping then that Richard might be calling, so I sort of hung around the door of the sunroom to hear. I could tell she was being invited somewhere. "Okay," she said just before she hung up. "I'll be ready at seven."

She looked up at me. "You wouldn't mind if I went out with Coach Pickle, would you? I wouldn't want you to feel uncomfortable about it."

"It's fine with me," I said. I did not tell her the whole date thing had sort of been my idea.

When Coach Pickle came to pick Rendi up, I was amazed. He had on nice slacks and a yellow shirt. There was no whistle around his neck. His hair was all combed, and he looked really good for a man his age. "I never thought I would be dating the principal's mother," he said just before they went out the door, and he winked at me.

I curled up on the couch for a long evening of phone conversation. Rendi had bought me a new cell phone, and I could call Katie and talk as long as I wanted on weekends. "What are you doing?" I asked when she answered, and she gave the usual reply. I told her all about Rendi's date and how nice Coach Pickle looked. We talked about Kash, who had actually called me on the phone twice during the week before and had asked me to go with his church when they went ice skating in Tulsa the next week.

Katie talked about her history project, and just before we hung up she said, "We got a new girl in our math class yesterday." I just made a grunting sound and waited because I could tell there was more. "Ivory wrote me a note right off about how absolutely dorky her clothes were."

"Good old Ivory," I said. I had given up trying to talk Katie into dumping the Six-Pack. I was always hoping, though, that she would.

"You know what?" said Katie. "On Monday, I am going to go over to the new girl before class and talk to her. If Ivory doesn't like it, so what?"

"Let me know how that turns out," I said.

Katie and I talked the next Saturday for a long time, but she never mentioned the new girl. I didn't ask because it was obvious that she had lost her nerve. Someday, though, she would break away from Ivory, and I was pretty sure it wouldn't be very much longer.

Life has settled down in Prairie Dog Town. I spend lots of time at the City Café. Would you believe the phone bill was five hundred dollars? From now on I'll get my psychic advice from fortune cookies. Mostly, I am Angie's assistant. She was pretty hard on me in the beginning. "Working here ain't going to be no latte," she told me on the first

* * * * *

day, but gradually she started to like me. I've even gotten used to her gum chewing, and sometimes Rendi will let me go to Ponca City with Angie to see a movie.

In the spring, there was a big unveiling of the statue Rendi had made for the town square. Lots of people came from art galleries, and there were newspaper people and even a television camera. My insides swelled with pride when they took the cover off the prairie dog. Oh, I guess most people would say that a prairie dog isn't nearly as big a deal as a pioneer woman, but I really felt that it was. For just a second, I closed my eyes, remembering the day we first drove into town. I opened my eyes to glance around me. The whole place looked so different to me now. It looked like home. Kash was standing beside me. I leaned over to him and whispered, "I love prairie dogs."